Who's Maria again?

MONA KRISTENSEN

ISBN 978-87-971033-5-7 (paperback 2021)
ISBN 978-87-974107-4-5 (hardback 2024)
Sequel in the book series: Becoming Maria.
The first, ”What's the Matter with Maria?”, was released in 2019.

Pot of Gold Publications
Copyright © Mona Kristensen

For the unique, immortal spark within,
which even after being blown nearly out or to bits,
may still be rekindled by the cradling hands of a caring heart

~ One ~

Living the dream

"Faster – hurry up or we'll never make it!!"

Drenched in sweat, Maria battles the grip of sleep. Her limbs feel kind of paralyzed. Disoriented, she opens her eyes, expecting to find the pink wallpaper in her bedroom at Matter Island before them. The walls here are white, however, and at some distance from Lisa's big bed, placed smack in the middle of a spacious bedroom with windows to the garden. Maria's eyes then land on Owly, sitting proudly at the foot of her bed. No need to keep her old cuddly friend under covers anymore.

Awareness awakens fully, and Maria exhales relieved. A sunflower of warmth unfolds its glowing petals inside her chest. It's vivifying.

Gee, what a peculiar, petrifying dream...

Maria was back by her old house, once again painting the fence. It mounted in front of her like an enormous wall, stretched high, high up in the air. All around her were these huge cans of paint; that same bluish-gray paint the villagers in her hometown Ferrysville like to use. Alas, Maria was ever so small in comparison: as tiny and downy as a baby bird. She tried to lift her right arm to get

1

going but couldn't move a muscle. Somehow, she knew it was beyond crucial to get the task done and fast. Her classmate Maggie, looking sort of shell-shocked, stood on the sideline, urging her on. Up high on the gable of their house, a giant clock was ticking with the insistency of a time bomb set to explode any second!

Yuck. Why are her dreams often so lifelike, feel tactile and tangible as waking reality? But thank god: she can move again. Maria reaches for her journal on the nightstand. It has become a habit to jot down dreams nearly every morning, besides everything else coming to mind. This one definitely needs to be noted!

Maria yawns, stretching her arms in the air. It's Saturday, no school or responsibilities to take care of. She can take her sweet time to wake up as mind and body love best.

She rests her head on the pillow. Outside, the sound of Spot barking and then Helen shushing him in her pretend-stern way puts a smile on Maria's face. It was probably what woke her up. Helen likes to sleep in, too, and she is likely annoyed about having to get up and let Spot out to do his business which is usually Jay's chore. Of course, an old dog needs to go more often in his senior years. It's good, he knows not to go after their hens.

Oh, she's had a great first year, here. Hard to believe, she's already on her second!

Since Maria moved, she's only visited her parents on Matter Island maybe four times, and by the day memories of Ferrysville and the hard-edged ways of the inhabitants on her native island slip further and further away. She's got other, much more fun things to ponder!

Mom likes to complain that Maria hardly ever calls them, and then she'll get a pang of conscience. The emotional state of her mother transfers frightfully fast through the wire. At times, she, to get off the hook, makes up excuses for hanging up sooner than necessary. Luckily, there's so much else going on in her life, that she doesn't have time to dwell on feelings of guilt. Not for long, anyway. Or Jay'll distract her ruminations, and she willingly lets him sway her focus in a more pleasant direction.

It so happens, that Jay isn't home right now. He and the rest of the choir jumped on a tour bus yesterday, and this afternoon they'll be singing in a cathedral in another big city across the country. Tomorrow is the first day of advent, December's fast approaching, and every single weekend until Christmas his choir is giving concerts.

Maria has no specific plans for today. Christine mentioned she might be dropping by this weekend, but she always has so many plans and things in the works outside school; you never know. Yesterday, Maggie, besides, asked Maria if she wanted to come to a casual Christmas party at her brother's flat, tonight? Maria, the youngest of the invited, hesitated and mumbled, "Uh, I don't know for sure, maybe..." It was a bit awkward. Hopefully, Maggie didn't feel offended.

It's just: she's only fourteen and the others are fifteen or older. Some of her classmates like to party at the weekends and on Mondays often joke about how drunk they were. Maria hasn't done any of such, yet. That frosh party at the end of August in her first year was super low-key and doesn't really count. Surely, Maria's mother still finds her daughter too young for partying and drinking? She expels the disconcerting dilemma from mind to think about matters lighter and easier to tackle.

Staying at Jay's grandparents' cottage is such a treat. Last year, they went to The Meadow Muse for all of the autumn holiday and this year, too. One whole week of eating well, going for long walks on the beach or in the nearby wild woods, reading books or enjoying different creative pursuits indoors. The Taylor family gathers at the cottage late Saturday afternoon after finishing up affairs in the city, making their first meal a casual but cozy potluck dinner. It's become a tradition.

The first time was special: Maria finally got to meet Jay's grandparents. After that unforeseen yet pleasant shock of recognizing his portrait, she'd been dying to meet Raymond.

She was so nervous, she was close to beside herself when Raymond stepped out of the car. The first part visible was the indispensable beret. No longer purple, though: on his silver-gray, still full head of wavy, windblown hair he sported a beret in bright orange. It glowed like a lighthouse at dusk. The sight instantly calmed Maria. A warm, tingly feeling arose inside. A lump in her throat.

Despite the huge age gap and most matters speaking against this being scientifically or otherwise possible, to **her** there's no question about it: Ray!

Jay's colorful grandpa looked shy and a little nonplussed. Raymond grabbed his wife's hand for support and had her take over while he gathered himself. Jay's grandma: a graceful woman with a youthful appearance and wise, calm eyes, greeted the likewise speechless girl with a sweet-scented hug and a peck on the cheek.

Emotional flashbacks rushed through Maria, as she stepped to-wards Ray.

They hugged each other lovingly, and Maria held onto him for a while to make sure the elderly man was real and wouldn't dis-solve in her arms. She felt dizzy, but he seemed solid enough. "How strange, indeed... I feel like I already know you well," Raymond mumbled, staring at her in awe. His, now gray instead of golden, eyebrows shot upwards as his face lit up in the familiar affection-ate and boyish smile.

Giddy, Maria leaned back, she couldn't stop laughing and Ray-mond soon joined in. Even his laugh sounded the same, the spirit of her old ally was still very much present somewhere inside his aging body.

"Come on now, you two! It's way too cold to be standing here chit-chatting: you have plenty of time to solve the "Grand Mys-tery" inside." Jay's grandma, Rose, shook her head with an impa-tient smile. She handed her husband a brown suitcase, grabbed a key in her sizable handbag and unlocked the door to the cottage.

As it turned out, this mystery is of the unsolvable kind. More like a knowing you feel deep within your bones but can't put into words, have no understandable language or proof to show for.

Raymond had, as Jay mentioned earlier, been close to leaving this earth-plane when he was little. For weeks he struggled with a severe case of tuberculosis and frightening fits of fever-delirium. He had been faint and wildly fantasizing but unable to, later on, recall any details from these feverish phantasms.

One thing, suggested a connection, though. When Ray finally got better, his parents, grateful for the much prayed for, miraculous recuperation of their son, wanted to buy him a special gift.

They asked him what his biggest wish was, and the weakened, yet again rosy-cheeked, kid promptly uttered that he absolutely needed to get hold of a Superman outfit! Only, his parents knew nothing of the airborne hero since the now-iconic Superhero wasn't to emerge on the scene until several years later...

It's a real puzzle and as such, the tender young girl and the eccentric old man decided to lay the riddle to rest and simply enjoy being reunited in this highly unexpected way, never for a second doubting their soul bond.

That autumn holiday turned out to be the best Maria ever had. The Meadow Muse proved able to live up to its lofty name! Every one of its residents felt invigorated, inspired to be creative on their own or in merry collaboration. She and Jay made a full quirky song including lyrics. Jay went as far as to record the sound of waves crashing onto shore, incorporating it in a way that sounded completely natural. Maria also, with instructions from Rose, created a ceramic cup that ended up slightly crooked. Still, she's okay content because after being burned in the oven, the glaze turned into a beautiful dusty pink. Now, she uses it daily for her favorite tea: a delicate blend, Rose has introduced her to.

Drinking tea from her own handmade cup has a special feel to it. A certain nobleness.

Still snuggled up in bed, Maria chuckles, bringing to mind a memory of Ray and Rose quietly bickering about the inappropriateness of wearing a beret indoors. Rose, shaking her head, stated that she refused to ever again dance with him wearing it. With a decisive movement, she fast snatched it from his head and threw it across the kitchen. It landed right on top of a ceramic bust of young Raymond made by herself years ago.

Everybody burst into laughter, and Raymond finally yielded. With a deprived face and a theatrical gesture, he grabbed his wife by her beret-tossing hand and twirled her across the floor in an impromptu tango.

~ Two ~

A new pair of boots

Maria gets out of bed and looks out into the backyard from her window.

Spot is running around out there among the flowerbeds, exploring and sniffing. To be a dog in this household is not too bad. To be a bonus child isn't, either...

She puts on her morning gown, a thick and fuzzy home-sewn birthday gift from her mother from her last visit at Matter Island. "It'll help keep you warm through the fall months," mom said with a motherly sigh, as the two of them wouldn't be seeing each other again till Christmas.

Maria strolls out into the kitchen where she finds Helen; or her "city mama" as Helen has aptly titled herself, sitting in front of the fireplace. As luck has it, the usually quite dynamic woman, just like Maria, prefers slow mornings. She gazes thoughtfully into the crackling flames while cradling a cup of coffee in her hands. There's a touch of sadness on her lit-up face.

Now that Lisa's gone, Helen sometimes complains about being the only extravert left in a household of "intolerable introversion", as she grins. How much Helen misses her eldest is apparent. After going off to university, Jay's big sister's hardly ever home: the grown girl tested her wings and left the safety of the nest, fully-fledged and fast.

Maria and Helen are getting along well. More often than not, Helen is attentive; like how she immediately got that her bonus daughter's first period was underway one evening when Maria was indisposed with stomach cramps. It felt a bit awkward, but they had a nice chat and afterward became closer. She knows she can talk to her city mama about pretty much everything. If Maria's able to get past her own insecurities, that is.

Every so often, a weak-kneed girl may worry if the country chick generously granted the flown bird's spot will be able to measure up...

"Good morning," Maria smiles and Helen looks up. "Oh, hi Maria! Or good morning I should say. I would've liked to sleep in, but Spot, of course, had to go. Did we wake you up, sweetie?" Maria nods, saying it's okay: she wants to make the most of the weekend.

She joins Helen by the fire and they chat cozily for well over an hour. Right until they're interrupted by Spot who has finally had enough of his adventures outside or maybe is freezing: he howls like a tiny miserable wolf by the patio door. Maria lets him in, only to be thanked by the villain jumping up and down; placing his dirty paws repeatedly on her soft gown. Wonder if the washing machine can take care of this?

Christian shows bleary-eyed up in the kitchen, where he hastily eats a bowl of granola. He played a gig last night and came home late. He's in a hurry since he's teaching a piano lesson in less than half an hour. "I desperately need a quick shower, before then," he yawns and disappears. Like his son, he'll often look absentminded, clearly engulfed in his own thoughts. He and Maria move somewhat shyly around one another but, as the sensitive introvert, they both are, also have a natural rapport.

The frequent and not always pleasant sound of someone plucking at the piano in the music room has been one of the hardest things to get used to for Maria in her new home. Christian's students, who are of all ages, start out by playing repetitious scales or repeating melody bits over and over and it can be tiring and a little stressful to listen to. She does use her earplugs a lot as suggested by Lisa.

Occasionally, Christian or one of his talented students plays delightful, riveting music, and if so, Maria leans her head against the wall in her bedroom on the other side, completely carried away.

Thank goodness, adapting to life in the suburbs has turned out to be fairly easy.

What she misses the most about Matter Island is its mellow landscape and having the forest and beach within walking distance. The Meadow Muse and the huge, magnificent natural reserve surrounding it, beat the scenery on her old island by far, but they only go there once or twice a month, tops.

Yep, Maria is still a country girl at heart and suspects she always will be. Nothing soothes and sets her easily overstimulated, easily rattled nervous system right, better than the tranquility of nature.

In winter, she'll sometimes have to take a crowded bus or train; something she detests, even if neither is as awful as how she felt on the rarer occasions, riding the subway... Whenever weather permits, Maria's served a nice dose of the specific nature available here: the suburban gardens and parks. Each morning on those days, she enjoys riding Lisa's chic pink bike, with its daisy-adorned wicker basket on the handlebars (and a lowered saddle), to school.

Besides the daisies, that basket has been holding quite a few flowers snatched from parks or even branches growing out of garden hedges: when it comes to her favorites, she just can't help herself! Helen's already made good use of Maria's love of flowers, noticing her knack for composing lovely combinations of colors, shapes and textures.

Weekly, she'll let the girl from the countryside arrange bouquets for their living room.

Most of the girls at school are city girls. Only Maggie, the one who looks kinda like her old neighbor and friend, Stella, comes from a smallish town in a rural area, too. She's got a tedious train commute to sit through every day and often seems tired. That's why she's starting to stay at her big brother Rick's place more: he's got a flat downtown with a spare room for guests sleeping over.

Maria is fond of Maggie. If you scratch the surface, you'll find a ravenous appetite for life burning beneath, easily overlooked at first glance. Her new girlfriend was only able to attend Fairview, which is a somewhat prestigious high school, because she was fortunate enough to receive a scholarship. And it only came about with the help of her old school's headmaster.

Neither of them lives in a dorm. She, who is one year younger than all her classmates, lives sheltered at the Taylors' house. Maria thinks Maggie's folks find their daughter still a bit too immature for that, but the two of them have never discussed the subject.

Yes, the girls have certain things in common: being a little less articulate than their classmates being one and the love of singing being another. Maggie's voice is seriously good: she's been singing ever since she was little, she says.

On the back wall of the school's atmospheric auditorium, a quote is written:

"Singing gives the heart wings & the world is starving for people with soaring hearts"

At morning assembly, students from all the creative wings at Fairview sing together; at times there's poetry reading, too. Maggie was once persuaded to take the mic and lead the lot of them. Despite being only a soph, she's just been chosen to play one of the biggest roles in the school's annual musical, next spring.

Maria treasures the daily dose of singing at Fairview: that phrase speaks truth.

Whenever Maggie sings, she becomes this totally different person, blissfully lost in baring her soul. There's such a heart-rendering note of melancholia in her voice: it gets Maria every time. When her talented classmate speaks, though, a slight lisp will now and then make her self-conscious. Most only find this peculiarity endearing. Aside from that, when either of them speaks in class, their sentences are fewer and farther between or come out a bit clunkier. In particular Maria's, of course.

She still loves the ambiance in their classroom. Warmth and light emanate, not only from the huge arched windows but equally as much from their inspiring teachers, especially Margaret, whose perceptive and powerful presence influences them daily. "The best art doesn't necessarily make logical sense, but you have to be able to feel it!" is one of the guidelines she's taught them.

Mr. Denman or someone of a similar dreary disposition, thank goodness, hasn't re-appeared and neither has any severe panic attacks. In the very beginning, a hint of fear might stir inside during lectures; especially if she started to feel somehow trapped. But since that day when Maria kind of snapped, Margaret's had her caring eye on her. They've had chats on anxiety, too, which has been comforting. Still, what helps more than anything is the relaxed atmosphere of calmness and kindness permeating this whole place as well as its people: a rare, but real lightness of being.

Plenty of wiggle room for Wonderers and Weirdoes!

Pupils at this preparatory school for a career in the Arts are a wonderfully varied lot of different ethnicity and background yet with a common thread of artistic sensibility. The most outwardly colorful are the ones from the Performing Arts department who take great pleasure in dramatically exerting their highly unique personalities. Though, there also are quite a few eccentric characters roaming the school's Music premises. Many a youngster around here swaps their hairstyle, clothes and overall outfit more often than the ordinary person changes toothbrush...

In comparison, her own style, along with her little quirks and foibles, seems bland.

Luckily, Maria fits okay amongst the literary types at the Creative Writing wing. It wasn't difficult for her to choose to head down this path at the end of freshman year. Maria did consider Visual Arts for a moment, but then she knew she wouldn't get to see much of Margaret. Like most of her fellow freshmen from introductory class, she gladly followed their beloved teacher into the world of words.

Pupils from this artistic department are amongst peers referred to as "lit nerds": a relatively mellow-tempered grouping who tend to act quieter or with a little more decorum. With exceptions, of course. Humans do not belong in boxes.

If Maria has a bad day, a stubborn feeling of being an out-of-place imposter creeps in. She'll then feel as if her classmates gaze, maybe not meanly but sorta mystified at her whenever she opens her mouth. Like was she speaking an unknown tongue, her awkward attempt at expressing herself hard to grasp.

In the privacy of her bedroom, Maria tries to catch up by reading or at least browsing through books fetched in Christian and Helen's office. It's quite big and with two big bookcases jam-packed with a diverse and varied collection of literature. She's positive that none of her classmates uses a dictionary as excessively as she does.

On good days, which far outnumbers bad ones, Maria realizes her worries are pure nonsense or simply that darned inferiority dragon messing with her head.

Margaret's steady mentorship is such a comfort: being under her teacher's wing helps loads. At first, Maria worried if the others noticed and disapproved, but their beloved teacher hands out interest and attention evenly and in generous amounts: everybody gets their share. Maggie and Maria have, besides, reached a silent understanding and always send each other an encouraging smile after awkward moments. It's seriously stress-reducing to have someone around who knows where you're coming from!

Some tuneless piano sounds wake Maria from her thoughts. No doubt, Christian is tutoring an absolute beginner today. The notes are off most of the time: any melody is hard to detect. She and Helen look at each other and chuckle. Then Maria gets up to wash her ceramic cup in the sink before jumping in the shower. She can't keep hanging about: important plans await this Saturday!

As streams of warm water flow down Maria's body, some twinklings trickle into her mind as well. What about creating a special, homemade gift for Jay this Christmas? There's plenty of time for working on it in secret, he won't be home much in the coming weekends: she could easily make it a surprise. Her mind digs into the details, pondering her idea.

A shower is as always the perfect place for receiving inspiration. It never fails. Although when she had just moved here, Maria would quite often cry in the shower, instead. Not because of unhappiness, even if she did feel homesick at first, rather out of sheer stress and overwhelm trying to adapt to all the newness. Water would flow from her eyes for a while, and the cathartic seance left her cleansed and calm, inside and out.

Early on, a template of urgency got hardwired into Maria. A way of being; pushing or stressing oneself, automatically and excessively, passed down through her bloodline. Replacing that old imprint with one of acting solely from natural inclinations and inspiration or else rest and rejuvenate, at first seemed to Maria as near blasphemous.

Now, she finally basks in the wellbeing this foundational shift brought about.

"True art, like true love, cannot be forced into existence," is Margaret's favorite phrase, "make a welcoming space within you for the muse to arrive, instead: woo it a little!" To notice and work with what bubbles up from deep inside is her primary teaching tool. She recently set forth a mini-course on fairy tales, showing them how these stories originate in a country's ancient myths and folklore and even when aimed at children are often profound or symbolic. This particular subject isn't every student's cup of tea: a couple of the boys yawn demonstratively. Maria is fascinated, though. She remembers the wonder she felt when reading some of them back on the island.

Last week, they wrote an essay on the topic. She dabbled at first but soon plunged merrily into those waters like a dolphin set free. Sentence after sentence poured out.

When she told about it at home, Jay was intrigued to the point of getting anxious. Maybe he shouldn't have chosen Fairview's music wing; creative writing is almost as interesting? Soon enough, he settled down. Coming up with words for song lyrics is also creative writing: through music, he gets the best of both art forms. Jay loves nothing more than exploring all kinds of, occasionally strange, sounds and geeking out on creating songs or evocative soundscapes. Composing **is** his thing.

Maria slowly puts on her clothes, undecided about what to do for the rest of the day. Maggie's face shows up in her mind's eye.

Didn't she look disappointed when Maria said maybe? The guilt-rut is so firmly furrowed in her brain, slipping back into it happens fast and without resistance. Despite recent insights, she still prefers when everyone around her is happy and content. It's mad, how conflicting desires between herself and others stress her out!

She decides to visit Maggie, thinking she can drop by on her bike and maybe invite her for a bite at a café. Again, Maria feels the sting of guilt for not saying yes right away to Maggie's invitation. She doesn't feel like going to that party, though, hasn't mentioned anything to Helen about it, either. Perhaps, if they hang out for a few hours this afternoon, Maggie won't feel hurt?

It's steaming hot in the bathroom. With steady fingers Maria draws a smiling face on the mirror and then wipes the condensation off it: a flushed face stares back with widened, worried-looking eyes. Helen knocks softly on the door, "Are you gonna be much longer, Maria? I would really like to get in there before driving off to do some shopping. Perhaps you'd like to come with me?"

"I'll be right out and yeah; a shopping trip sounds fun!" Maria quickly wraps a towel around her dripping wet, unruly reddish hair which she daily, to little avail, works to flatten or, at the least, tame. She steps out of the room. "Not the mall, I guess?" Helen smiles at her. "Oh no, pedestrian street, definitely pedestrian street!" no explanation is necessary. Jay's mom, needless to say, gets the preference of her household's most recent introvert.

Three hours later the two shopping gals eat late lunch at a café with loads of bags surrounding their table, of which some contain holiday presents. After their meal, they make one last stop at a posh shoe shop. Helen insists on buying a pair of winter boots for Maria: an offer she, after a bit of polite protest, happily accepts. "See it as our Christmas gift for you," Helen smiles. They're so smart in a warm maroon color: knee-high and with high heels, too! Thrilled, Maria brushes a flash of her mother's self-effacing face off her mind and decides to keep them on.

She looks and feels taller, all grown-up, as she strolls beside Helen in her new boots. Maria's city-mama squeezes her shoulder with an acknowledging smile.

It's a sunny day and pedestrian street is crowded today, mostly by fresh-faced, lively chatting teenage girls with long shiny hair which they often in a self-assured manner toss about, laughing to their similar-acting girlfriends. It strikes Maria, how she, at least seen from outside, might fit into that category, herself. Not a bad box to inhabit! Didn't she perhaps get an A on the first essay they've been graded on, only last week? Margaret praised her for it: "A sensitive piece laden with emotion - excellent work!" Straightening her spine, Maria lifts her head as a sense of pride and pure, undiluted joie de vivre shoots through her.

In the spur of the moment, Maria tells Helen about the Christmas party tonight and Maggie's invitation. And Helen, who of course knows of Maggie and likes her well, says that if only Maria's mother is okay with her going, it'll be fine by her, too. Maria should call her mom to ask and get back to Helen on when she wants to be fetched. "It's only a ten-minute drive. Hubby and I'll probably be up until midnight anyway," Helen nodded.

Maria's mom seemed stressed and clearly had Christmas preparations and expenses on her mind, she only hesitated a second before giving the green light. Maria felt another sting of guilt and kept quiet about her new boots. When Helen late in the afternoon drops Maria off at Rick's place, their cozy chit-chatting in the car

has lifted her mood. Also, she's wearing a lavender tunic with silver piping in Helen's becoming design - her first party in the city
awaits!

As Maria presses the door buzzer, a few light-sleeping butterflies wake up inside her stomach and start fluttering about. She's
never been here before, never met Maggie's older brother.

Most strangers still scare her at first.

Still life of the party

Maria sees it coming from across the room.

That guy is definitely heading in her direction. He aims straight
for the end of the couch where she's squeezed in, halfway hidden
behind Rick. Maggie's easy-going, burly brother is currently engaged in passionate conversation with a curvaceous girl in black
tights, a short grey skirt and a low cut off-white satin top. Maria
looks around but there's no sight of Maggie anywhere, no one to
turn to for escape.

"Come on, don't be such a party pooper - let's dance!" the eager, young man's mouth is wide-open, reading his lips is easy. He
is clearly close to shouting, but the noise of laughing people and
loud thumping music from a loudspeaker in the corner right behind her drowns out his words. It looks a bit uncanny, mirroring
how she feels.

About a dozen grinning, more or less intoxicated teenagers bob their heads, of which many are clad in Santa-hats, and sway their limbs to the rhythmic music out on the floor. Maggie's brother and a couple of others moved the dining table and chairs to make room to dance.

Maria's heart beats fast, she feels flustered and insecure. Where on earth is Maggie when you need her?

Her absent, potentially soon-to-be Bff has made a cozy nest for herself in Rick's spare room with a lovely bedspread, purple candles, fairy lights around the mirror and feminine decor. She and Maggie have been chit-chatting about school and other vital, personal matters all afternoon, getting to know one another better. Maggie has also taught the younger teen how to put a perfect eyeliner on to create dramatic eyes; she always looks so cool herself.

The fifteen-year-old girl's got big dreams, "You know, my real, full name is actually Magdalena after my father's mother. My family's always called me Maggie, though, because it sounds more modern, cuter or whatever. But Magdalena is going to be my stage name!"

Watching her perform a sad song she's written herself, Maria's convinced her talented classmate's dream will come true. In her own way, Maggie totally nailed that tune!

They had great fun comparing experiences of being country girls in the city. Maggie is a straightforward kinda girl and candidly shared her most embarrassing moments. Soon, she had Maria in tears with a belly ache from laughing so hard. At one point the former islander even fell off the bed!

Later, they had pizza by the dining table, ordered and paid for by Rick. They laughed about how wonderfully un-christmassy eating pizza was. His living room appears rather vacant, furnished only with a big, expensive-looking oak wood dining table, six matching chairs and a set of leather sofas. In a corner, there's a plastic Christmas tree with beaming multi-colored lights. The walls and window sills are empty, however. No posters, plants and pillows; basically none of those trinkets or personal details that make a place feel like home.

Maria, who doesn't know this twenty-something fellow at all, felt shy and nervous. Maggie and her brother both nonchalantly grabbed a beer and offered one to Maria who accepted, tasting it for the first time. She didn't like its bitter taste much and only took tiny sips. The beverage pleasantly calmed her nerves, though.

Maggie and Rick seem close. They're flippant with each other and bicker in that non-serious manner siblings often do. Rick likes to tell Maggie what to do, and she likes to question or poke fun at most of his unsolicited brotherly advice yet clearly looks up to him anyhow. There can be no doubt about their blood ties.

Young people, some with clinking plastic bags in their hands, started dropping in, each one greeted heartily by Rick. Maggie quickly put more drinking glass on the table. Maria gazed at the foreign faces, greeting each one with a happy "hi!", too. She felt warm and relaxed. Included.

These last drops are flat and lukewarm. Maria has only had a couple of beers tonight, sipping on it for a long time. She's been readying herself to go phone Helen, but she feels a bit lightheaded and woozy. It's been so amusing watching the others party all evening, safely observing them from behind Rick's back. This sofa is, besides, slippery and hard to leave, especially after realizing she has to walk across the room to reach the hallway, zig-zagging in between bouncing youngsters.

And now this tall, blond and good-looking guy is standing there, asking **her** to dance!

Maria peeks up at him through her curtainy bangs, shaking her head profusely with an apologetic smile. "Argh, just forget it, you're nothing but a baby!" he shrugs, staring brazen-faced at her flat chest with its budding blinis behind the tunic's flimsy fabric. The blunt fellow aims his tentacles at a more accommodating target; the piercing blue eyes fast scan the area. Displaying a strong wrist with a chain-tattoo, he grabs the girl next to Rick by the hand and swiftly drags her, uninhibitedly grinning, away from the sofa accompanied by loud protests from his pal.

Waves of shame flush through Maria, she rises fast from the sticky black leather. A red-cheeked Bambi on unsteady high-heeled feet, she rushes across the floor, clumsily making her way around swaying hips and flailing arms. Once safe in the hallway, she grasps the knob on the bathroom door, with a thump trying to get in, but it's locked.

"All right, all right! I'm on my way, already, geez..." Maggie's words are slurred. When she opens the door and sees Maria, she laughing pulls her flustered friend inside and locks the door again. "Pleeaase don't tell Rick, but I just threw up," Maggie chortles childishly. "Don't worry, I am better now," she reassures, pressing a hand against her mouth, "great party, eh? even if I actually don't know half of these people. But some veeery cute guys! Especially Gregg... you know the tall blond with striking blue eyes and a tattoo on his wrist? Oh boy, is he yummy!"

Maria nods, uncertain about how to handle these confessions, "Yeah... but isn't Gregg kinda old? Like, almost grown-up?" Maggie straightens her back, "I prefer older guys. The boys at school are okay, I guess. Well, they're *boys*, you know?" she squints at Maria, her face shrewd. "I know Gregg from back home: his family lives only a few blocks from ours. He and Rick move in the same circles. He's **so** cool: plays in this great band with a super cute singer, Marcus. Those guys are gonna go far, I tell ya!" Maggie's voice is intense, then her tone shifts: "gosh, sometimes I forget you're still only fourteen, Maria. One year changes a LOT."

The phone rings outside in the hallway, right beside the door, interrupting their chat. It's probably Helen. Relieved, Maria hastily unlocks the door and answers it.

Luckily, it **is** Helen. "Can I pick you up now? she asks, "it's almost midnight and I'm ready for bed." Maria's only happy to accommodate her request and 15 minutes later sits comfortably in the passenger seat on their way home. "Did you and Maggie have a good time at the party; did you dance? I hope the young people were behaving?" Helen, yawning, wants to know.

"I didn't feel like dancing but yeah, we had a great time," Maria nods, telling about Maggie's cozy room, Rick's empty apartment and their unseasonable yet satisfying pizza-eating, not feeling like giving any more details.

For once, Helen is quiet, too sleepy to question further.

~ Three ~

Vacation on Matter Island

Tiny droplets hit Maria's face: a drizzle of salt-tasting rain. Facing the roaring north wind while gazing across a body of water from the deck of a ferry stirs up memories. All kinds of feelings run through her in ripples and waves, imitating the sea.

This huge streamlined one and the rickety old "Nuisance" from Matter Island don't have much in common, though, besides sharing the term ferry and a somewhat similar form. Maria pulls the collar on her coat tighter around her neck and takes one last glance at the ocean before heading toward the stairs to the cafeteria. Once inside, she quickly makes her way amongst a lot of chatting, lunching travelers to the only vacant table and sits down, suddenly feeling awfully and awkwardly alone.

It would've been a nice gesture if Jay had joined her. Maria's parents have invited him several times, yet he always declines; politely but firmly. His dislike for the island is obvious. Always such a contrarian... Isn't Jay behaving a little too demonstrative? Surely, **most** islanders are friendly!

Although her thoughts awaken slight anger, it's not enough to heat up Maria's chilled body. She's freezing but nonetheless feels too shy to order a hot drink in the cafeteria. Maria stares at her hands on top of the waxed tablecloth: they're so small and almost blue now. She puts them in her coat pockets under the table.

Both Helen and Maria's parents were pressed for time in the busy days preceding the holidays and arranged to share the task of transporting Maria to Matter Island for her Christmas stay. Oceans surround their country on most sides, and Helen suggested dropping her off by a fast ferry port only one hour's drive from the capital city, and then her parents could pick her up on the other side less than a two-hour drive from the island. Maria, afraid to be a burden, agreed to their deal. This way the only bridge to cross is the new one to Matter Island, erected only last summer.

After Maria's fetched at the ferry port, the black station wagon drives steadily across the winter-colored mainland to sweep fast over the brand new bridge. The familiar landscape on the island emerges. It looks different to Maria: still picturesque in places but somehow also smaller and flatter.

Back at her childhood home, no Leo greets her with overjoyed barking or carrying a random piece of footwear in his mouth. This fall, her parents had to put him to sleep, mom explains: the old lab's heart was done. Maria feels his absence like a ghost in the house, shedding some tears. "Yes, Leo is sorely missed..." her mother's eyes sadden.

She shakes it off, noticing Maria's shiny new boots, "When did you get those? They're quite chic even if not exactly practical..." staring at them, she suddenly looks miffed, mumbling about not needing any acts of charity, "we're fully capable of clothing our own daughter, thank you very much!" Maria hurries to say the boots are a Christmas gift from Helen and Christian, an impulse buy. Downplaying the matter, she swiftly moves on to other topics.

Better not mention that this isn't the first time Helen has kindly bought Maria something cool for her wardrobe...

No bad vibes are to be created between the two most important women in her life!

Fortunately, her father steps through the doorway to their kitchen. While he doesn't seem to care about what Maria is wearing, he does mention she looks taller. "What on earth are the people feeding you over there, or is perhaps the waterworks in the city secretly adding fertilizer to the water, eh?" dad grins with his characteristic wink. Neither he nor mom has changed much since Maria's last visit, except the fact that dad's mustache is gone which makes her father appear weirdly boyish.

After a short time, John cuts in with ramblings about school. The second grader's got a lot to tell his sister after not seeing her for months, and in his eagerness pulls so hard at one of her sleeves that its lace trimming unravels. "Oh no!" Maria inspects the rift, "Helen made this for me, only last week." John goes quiet but only for a second, "I almost didn't touch it, mom, I swear!" he gazes agitated at their mother, who shakes her head, "Well, she **is** clever our Helen, but maybe her designs are a bit too flimsy for country living. Although fancy designs are fun to make, Lilian, our boss at the sewing workshop, always makes sure to add a healthy dose of practicality to our off-the-rack collections. We have to take the market on Matter Island into consideration, not least in winter. Such a thin blouse is both rather revealing as well as hardly able to keep you warm, Maria?"

Her daughter can't deny this. She is, in fact, still freezing and retreats to her bedroom, which is in the process of being made into a sewing room, to put on a warm sweater.

The delicate top has to be saved for when Maria's back in the city.

Her old room is completely changed. The wallpaper's still that same pink one, but otherwise, not much is recognizable. Her mother has placed a huge desk up against the window for her sewing machine, and dad has put up shelves on the wall beside it: they're filled with fabric, scissors, many rolls of yarn or thread and all sorts of sewing equipment. Maria's bedroom is clearly transforming into her mother's dream version of a sewing room. All of Maria's toys, stuffed animals, knick-knacks and posters are gone, probably exiled to the basement.

She pictures several boxes of childhood treasures down there, all of them tagged with mom's neat handwriting and completely covered in cobwebs.

Maria feels deprived for a moment and fights off a sense of sadness. It didn't take her mother long... Her conscience comes rushing back. It's good to know mom's reunited with her sewing machine, just like when Maria was little. She recalls how much she admired mom for her craftwork back then: all those cuddly toys and cute creations. It was her very first glimpse into understanding the power of creativity. For years, mom hasn't had a room of her own. Not since John was born.

At least, Maria's bed is still in there.

Back by the kitchen table with her family, she speaks warmly of mom's sewing skills as a low winter sun breaks through a lead grey, overcast sky and lights up everything in its merciless rays. Maria notices how shabby the cupboards look and how stained the stove; just how outdated and dingy the vinyl floor is. How the refrigerator door, by now, is more yellow than white, even if its surface is hidden behind notes, magnets with sunny affirmations and crawl gnomes. Mom's excessive Christmas decor cannot hide what Maria hasn't dared admit to herself before, what she hoped her mom's new job and her dad getting a better one might have taken care of. Maybe keeping her at Fairview is expensive..?

Maria is happy when the sun disappears behind clouds again.

As usual, her parents ask questions about life in the city. Mom looks impressed half of the time and the other half lets out a word of warning.

"It's just so different there," Maria gushes, "the other day, we visited the city's world-famous art museum. I loved the paintings from the impressionistic era: the color palettes they used were so vibrant and alive; like luminous!"

Silence. Wryly, dad winks to mom, "Huh, listen to our little girl; isn't she beginning to sound a right mini Helen...?" his tone is as dry as the sand on Matter island shores.
Maria blushes, biting her lip. Looking down, she notices a sizable dust bunny under her dad's chair, right next to one of his slippers. She puts all of her focus on it.

Her father wants assurance his daughter is behaving and besides makes her promise to never ride her bike alone late at night through the sinister city streets downtown teeming with dangerous gangs, pushers and prostitutes. "Even we backward islanders watch the News, you know. That's a nasty environment," he preaches. "Yes, I've seen enough awful things on those "Real Crimes" TV shows!" her mother agitated chirps in. Her father grins, teasingly stating how Maria is unlikely to become a hardcore criminal in a matter of months. Mom part sighs, part hisses and rises from her seat to clear the table. Maria relaxes and laughs along.

The Holidays rush by in the wink of an eye.

On Christmas Eve: this year a more green than white one, Maria catches up with her grandparents and the extended family. Everything is per usual, down to the big bowl of apples and oranges in the hallway and the constant babbling of her chatty younger cousins. Her older cousins are curious about Maria's surprising move to the city and what it entails. Stretched between feeling pride for being considered interesting and acute shyness about the attention, Maria answers as best she can.

Louise can't hide her envy, "If only mom and dad would let **me** do anything remotely as exciting as that. This island is dragging me down! No cool shops or cozy cafés, nothing but that boring old snack bar at the marina. Business school is ok, I guess, but then where do I go next? Apprenticeship at the Women's Daily-wear shop in a town lousy 7 miles away isn't exactly my idea of adventure…"

Maria doesn't know what to say and so simply nods in sympathy. Being put in the spotlight and seen as someone who daringly steps onto foreign and even first-rate territory is untrodden land for her. An alluring role and repute, she must admit.

Later on, gifts are distributed with generous hands. Maria, with so much else going on in her life, hasn't had the wits about her to wish for anything in particular. She's a wee bit disappointed when unwrapping her parents' present for her. It's a heather gray blazer in a flecked fabric, sewed by her mother. The blazer has many nice details, like seamed pockets on the outside as well as one hidden in the lining. Her mom proudly informs that it took her hours to sew: this fabric is top-notch, she finishes. The design is to the old-fashioned side and hangs like a sack on Maria who hasn't got the heart to say so. Praising her mother's skills and dexterity, she avoids overtly lying as well as mom's earnest eyes by hugging her warmly as thanks.

Hugging is still awkward, but mom's face lights up.

The days after Christmas are mellow and restful. Everybody eats way too much of those rich and sugary holiday dishes and, as usual, ends up complaining about tummy aches or acid reflux. On Boxing Day's evening Maria's mom; wiped out after weeks of cleaning, baking and cooking, makes remarks about all the time and money she's put into meeting the crazy demands of this overindulgent time of year, only to get poor responses. Dad jokingly suggests she can pick up some boxes of Mr. Price's Fishy Sea Fruits from the freezer for the next couple of days.

Turns out, their freezer is still chock-full of his old boss' brand of fish since dad was offered a lot for free after the guy fell ill last summer and was forced to retire.

It's strange to think of how the old fish factory is shut down now.

Maria hasn't been visiting the harbor for some time. Tomorrow, however, they'll go for a brisk, long walk and take a look at what's been changing in Ferrysville while she's been away. For one, the convenience store next door has expanded its space and capacity into a fully-stocked Mini Market with the catchphrase "All the best for prices less", much to the grocer's great pride. Opening hours have expanded as well, "One has to keep up with the demands of modern-day consumers," their neighbor claims.

Down at the building site, Bill clearly hasn't been beating around the bush, either: the large and hideous concrete plant is in the midst of a radical transformation. They're reconstructing it into a shipyard where the biggest fishing boats are remodeled into highly modern sightseeing ships for tourists, dad informs. Every single part of the interior structure has been removed, including the asbestos ceiling, to make room for it to house such grand vessels under its roof, while the exterior walls are clad with beautiful greyish green larch planks now. The fish factory is unrecognizable.

It's a mild winter day with close to no wind, and a few young people as well as the previous factory owner Mr. Price tucked under a checkered blanket in his wheelchair are gathered, engaged in conversation. Maria notices the grocer's oldest daughter Susan standing beside Jack and Bill who, it seems, is the one pushing his invalid old man today. Her stomach sinks. Then Maria catches herself and takes a deep breath, straightening her back: no need to be afraid of these folks, anymore. She approaches them with a big smile, nodding to her childhood friend as well as the pair of freshly converted foes.

"Hi Maria - long time, no see!" Susan seems pleased to see her, "Merry Christmas from those of us stuck here in smelly old "Fishyville", the perky young woman grins at the age-old pun. She looks at her boyfriend who shakes his head while softly pulling at her ponytail. "Better come up with a better nickname, soon, hon: by summer, selling questionable fish is no longer what this lil ol' town will be famous for!" The two of them are clearly the smitten kittens, still.

Maria sends Mr. Price a semi-frightened glance. Won't he be offended by such disrespect from his own son and maybe soon-to-be daughter-in-law? The gnarly guy certainly would've been a year and a half ago. But now, he stares absently into space, a consistent tiny smile creating a blissed-out expression. The features of his weathered face have softened: the callous man's uncompromising mindset is nowhere to detect. Whatever caused this sea change, something is dawning on Maria.

An exhausting era ruled by Patrick Price's agenda, driven by his insatiable hunger for profit and power seems to finally be over. For good and for real.

That same night lying in bed, she tries to come to grips with the myriad of ways her life's changed these last eighteen months. All for the better, yet there's unrest inside.

What devils do a hypervigilant body and busy brain watch out for after the one who played a key part in forming both apparently has been dethroned?

From now on, maybe her friends are real and enemies, imaginary?

~ Four ~

Small-town girls united

Back in the city, heydays follow the Christmas party at Rick's place.

In early January, the two girls start hanging out all the time. To sit next to Maria, Maggie switches seats with Christine which is no big deal: the pupils' seatings are fluid, not fixed.

Nearly a decade of swimming in the lukewarm waters of solitude turns around for Maria, propelling her into a riveting and pleasant flow of ease: a joint flow able to flush away any obstacle. She almost can't believe such a miracle!

And as for Maggie; her confidence steadily grows, nourished by Maria's affection and admiration. She's openhearted and forthright once you get to know her. Underneath the surface shyness worn as protection, she's full of beans, quick-witted and curious about the world, in particular the odd ways of its crazy occupants. Maggie likes to, with a knowing face, let her younger friend in on her opinions and observations. She is, after all, merely from the outlying suburbs; not from some remote island.

That is already one step ahead.

Maggie is easy to talk to, no effort is needed in their interactions: they simply click. Feeling safe, Maria finally lets her guard down. It feels so good to have a like-minded girlfriend, at last: a trusted confidante of the same gender and, almost, age to share her secrets with.

Frequently, the two teen girls' lust for life and playful curiosity spill over and fits of uncontrollable laughter sound from their corner of the classroom. Eric, a whip-smart, self-proclaimed wordsmith, fast comes up with a suitable moniker: "The Dotty Duo". Most of their jestful classmates play along, more than willing to follow his lead.

Soon after, Maggie starts terming Maria "homegirl", and every single time, she gets a fuzzy feeling inside: a gratifying sense of belonging. To reciprocate she'll now refer to her new friend as "Mag" because giving a special person a special name is endearing!

When Maria thinks of this affinity between them, she feels certain that the common ground they spring from is a rock-solid foundation for their blossoming friendship: an unbreakable fortress withstanding any storm.

The last few months have been magical. The two of them have been as close as Maria's ever been with another girl. To gaze into Maggie's beaming, oceanlike eyes where emotions rise and retract in engulfing waves, mirrors back an alluring, lucent hue she only recalls experiencing in her happiest dreams or perhaps as a bubbly, carefree toddler. Sparks fly from them, catching on like wildfire inside Maria.

Only seldom does Maggie share about her home-life.

Rick was quick to escape to the city or: "get the hell out of that house," as he bluntly says, encouraging his sister to do the same. By now, Maggie is pretty much moved into her big brother's apartment, and he now, to his little sister's part amusement, part annoyance, tries to act as a father figure, even if a half-baked one. Rick seems to enjoy asserting parental powers now and then, even if he bemoans it, "Dad's gone and mom doesn't want to be the bad guy, so I guess, I have to."

There have been more parties there, too, since that one in December, and Maria has slept over a few times which took a bit convincing Maria's mother, but on one critical call, Rick grabbed the phone and with suaveness diverted her anxious ramblings. Seems, a manly voice uttering quasi-philosophical phrases on how children mature earlier nowadays and do well with responsibility did the trick of calming her mom's nerves.

They've had no problems since.

And what is okay with Maria's mother, is, by and large, okay with Helen, too. In fact, Jay is the only one who's been a bit standoffish toward Maggie.

Like every year, the Taylors spent Easter at The Meadow Muse. Maria invited her new Bff which was fine by Jay's grandparents: there's plenty of room in the cottage.
Everybody was charmed by the talkative teenage girl, and Rose laughed that they would consider it when Maggie suggested leaving "The" out of the name of their homestead to make it sound more modern.

Only Mag and Jay didn't exactly hit it off, and Maria hasn't got a clue why.

The whole time, Jay tinkered with some music project alone, even if Maria tried to get him included in their conversation. Or she would catch him gazing at the two of them; chatting and laughing, with a puzzled, at times, brooding look. Only when, on the last evening, enticed by Helen, Mag sang one of her main songs from the spring musical for them, his face lit up and he joined his father by the piano to accompany her. Maggie, clearly feeling right at home, gave her all: both hands swayed gracefully and finger-tips softly painted the melody with dots in the air. She delivered the song so effortlessly, tinged with a tonal palette of emotions. It sounded amazing!

Ray and Helen applauded and cheered and Maria even whis-tled. With the concert only a month away, Mag could use every ounce of encouragement.

"For a girl with a voice like hers, the sky must be the limit!" even Rose was in awe, and earning the gracious lady's accolade is not an easy accomplishment, Maria senses.

Yet, a few days later, Jay muttered something about having a bad feeling about Mag, "Maggie's got a gift, sure, even if I, hon-estly, could easily imagine her squandering it... Does it mean you have to stop singing yourself and always hang on her lips, though? Not every word she lets out is pure gold..." Maria got mad, proba-bly he's just sulking because the spotlight, for once, wasn't aimed at him. As usual, he is super busy with his music, friends, choir practice, tours and what have you. Lucky for Maria, she found someone else who's got room in their schedule for her!

Despite their, by now, close-knitted sisterhood, it can be a bit hard to come by what precisely the trouble is at Maggie's house.

If touching on it, the eyes of Maria's new Bff glaze over and she shakes her head. She merely hints at things like her parents arguing or she'll complain about dirty dishes in the sink and a messy living room.

Once, asked directly, Maggie opened up more, "After my grandmother died of breast cancer last year, dad has kinda lost it. It happened so fast and to make matters worse, mom's clueless on how to help. Well, we all are," her voice, uncharacteristically thin and vulnerable, quivered, "I just wanna forget about it. From now on, I only wanna focus on my bright future... Let's only do that, please?"

Maria felt tight around her chest. Choked, she nodded with a gentle smile. They moved on to other topics.

A crucial part of Maggie's bright future is her new, if things go as she plans, boyfriend Gregg. The talk often revolves around him. The stunner is almost twenty, 6 foot 2 and plays bass in a real band: a cool one named Vanguard Villains that plays upbeat pop music with a rockish edge. The band consists of four guys and two backing choir girls, and their lead singer's a young guy named Marcus. They're creating a lot of buzz right now and on the brink of a breakthrough, the rumor goes. A famous music magazine named them the next big thing: *the* up-and-coming new act this year. Gregg recently promised Maggie that she can sing with them occasionally if one of their regular girls is absent; she's got the pipes for it. He alluded to how she might even replace one of them soon **if** she keeps it on the low down and practices hard.

With such an advantageous prospect, Maggie's interest in their school projects, apart from the spring concert, is naturally starting to decline a smidgen.

Stage frenzy

During the next month, life at Fairview is turned upside down.

There's an excited buzz in the air, as the varying pieces of this popular annual event, steadily and with only minor mishaps, are put into place. As usual, interdisciplinary art forms with students from all different creative wings collaborate to ensure success. The size of the audience is expected to be significant; not merely parents and family but citizens from all over town. A notorious reviewer from the metropolitan paper is said to be coming as well.

If she gets a flattering mention, Vanguard Villains will switch things up, Mag is sure.

Everyone in the cast and crew is gifted a few free tickets to the show, and she has handed out hers to Gregg and Marcus, in case they feel like going. Since Jay likely won't be interested, and Lisa currently is located in Paris as an exchange student, Maria hasn't had anyone to give her spare ones to. The two tickets still lie in a pocket of her school bag, wrinkle-free.

"Argh, it's too much - my nerves can't handle it!" Mag moans as time draws close. She, nevertheless, looks healthier than ever. To commiserate with her, Maria, after a flutter of apprehension, starts sharing about her own bouts of social anxiety, but Mag cuts in: "Yeah, yeah, everybody gets nervous: it's totally normal. I know that! But these stage jitters are on a whole other level, I kid you not..." shrugging, she goes on, telling in details how she threw up before her first few auditions," dad says not to dwell on my anxiety but put all the focus doggedly on performing, instead. It's just so hard!"

Maria helps her Bff calm down as best she can, reinforced in the belief that shying away from the spotlight herself is the only option for someone of her skittish nature.

After rehearsals at school, they continue rehearsing all her lines and songs in Maria's bedroom. The Taylors are way more tolerant than Rick who, besides, claims to be totally tone-deaf: for that same reason, Maggie's brother probably won't be coming to the concert. But whenever Helen's got time, she kindly offers a listening ear, although yawning reveals how sleep-deprived she's getting as one of three main musical leaders, in charge of singing.

Jay, on the contrary, is elsewhere engaged and never home...

Many stage-players are, naturally, from the Performing Arts wing, but lots of other skills are required. Three weeks before the concert date, Michelle from the musical crew recruits Maria, among others, to put her drawing skills to good use and help in making backdrops and scenery.

One key scene takes place by a riverbank surrounded by flowers, grasses and reeds: right up her alley! She draws some sketches and templates at home which turns out all right and luckily gets accepted. Maria collaborates with the steady-handed Christine and a few others from the Visual Arts department to enlarge templates, outline and paint the malleable plywood in vivid colors. Lastly, they're erected and fastened by handy guys from the crew. The staging folks spontaneously applaud: this botanical style fits perfectly.

Even if Maria is stressed to the max, this is incomparably the coolest thing she's ever been part of!

To support her, by now almost cockeyed, stage-debuting friend, Maria promises to cheer Mag on from backstage. She'll be behind the scene, ready to help her relax in between scenes and at intermission. If she thinks too much about it, Maria feels sad she won't be in front of the stage, enjoying the show from a soft chair like the rest of the audience. On the other hand, feeling stuck within a large crowd still makes her anxious: this way, everything works out.

Days fly by, before they know of it, the evening of the premiere arrives.

The windows of the modern concert hall, just across the street from Fairview, glow in golden reflections of the powerful spring sun as family members, good friends of the performers and fancily dressed city folks in small groups enter the dimly lit music hall.

While excitement for the show slowly builds in front of the scene, a different drama unfolds behind it.

"Come on Mag, you know these songs like the back of your hand now - you've got this!" with her head close to the wooden toilet door, Maria speaks in an encouraging voice, hoping she sounds calmer than she feels. The bustle and buzzing noise from people outside get louder, but that's because a warm-up act of talented young guys; among others, Eric, will be performing a skit before the concert. There's still well over an hour to curtain draw for the main show.

Maria sends out a thankful thought to whoever gave her the hunch to meet up with Mag extra early: before the rest of the cast and Helen arrive.

When she got in a few minutes past five o'clock, the girls' dressing room was empty: no Maggie. As the time passed, panic started rising like a tidal wave inside. Then she detected a sniffle from the far end toilet booth and instantly knew what was going on. The foreboding became familiar and a comforting calm fell upon her.

At first, the only response Maria gets from the other side of the door is a choked-up mutter. "I can't do it. It's too hard – I just can't!"

"Come on, Mag: **no one** around here can sing like you do, it's amazing," Maria lowers her voice to a tender, insistent whisper, her lips near the keyhole. "H-how do you know I won't forget every single line? Or fall flat on my face in front of everyone?" Mag half cries, "that would be so typically me!" As always when upset, her lisp gets extra distinct, then her voice cracks followed by loud sobbing.

"And what about all those auditions you've been to, then? I would never dare to do something like that: don't forget how brave you are. The whole of Fairview believes in you and Gregg does, too: everybody believes in you!" Maria reminds her.

"Not everybody! Gregg said he wasn't sure if they had time for it... and dad doesn't care enough to come, and he even does this sort of thing for a living," Mag cries. She must be drinking; there's a clinking sound as a bottle lands on the mosaic-tiled floor.
"You know, my grandma was once a singer, too. When dad was a teenager, she sang at
Community halls, village pubs and such. But grandpa didn't like it and then she quit. She was good. I know, because when I was lit-

tle, she would every so often sing with me when we were on our own... see: singing runs in the family!" Maggie sniffles.

Maria bites her lip as a pang in her chest moves on to her throat. She inhales deeply. It's true, Maggie's father won't be coming tonight, only her mother; she told so yesterday with a shrug: "He's too busy or whatever... who cares."

"Look, forget about that old story, Mag. This is now and **he** is the one missing out on greatness: it is **his** loss. Pretend there's no audience and you're only singing for me. Forget about everybody else, this is **your** night. Do this for me, instead, or better yet; do it for yourself. *Do it because this is what brings you ALIVE: because it is YOUR thing!*" the right words suddenly find Maria.

A speck of light sparkles and glitters at the periphery of her eyesight. Claire is back, clearer and stronger than ever. An unexpected rush of joy shoots through her.

For a moment, it's dead silent behind the locked door. Maria's heart drops again.

Then she hears Maggie tear off some toilet paper and blow her nose. She gets on her feet, by the sound of it, in a less than elegant way while the door opens without a squeak: it is, after all, brand new. The leading lady in-spe is already dressed up for the first scene but her face is, apart from the nose, pale and unpainted, eyes moist. Mag looks frail and naked. Sober, in spite of the liquor.

Maria hugs Maggie warmly. "Hopefully, you haven't been drinking too much of that stuff?" she nods toward the bottle in her girlfriend's hand. The booze is disguised as another beverage: one they both know it's not. Mag smiles apologetically, "Nah, only a few sips. I just needed a little fortifier to get me through, you know..." she sighs and screws the cap back on. Not tightly, though.

"You've got me for that," Maria squeezes her shoulder encouraging, secretly a little surprised about how fast her words worked. A sense of weariness descends upon her. To fight it off, she straightens up and smiles big, "I'll go fetch a cup of coffee from the vending machine, it'll freshen you up," Maria rushes out, bumping into Helen in the doorway.

"Well, hello – there you are! When you didn't show up at the back entrance like the rest, I wondered where you were! Should've known the two of you would be in for a head start. Your dedication is impressive!" Helen, along with the cast of other girls, slide fast past her, nervously chatting yet in high spirits.

On stage, the young comedians' skit generates roars of laughter. To such a soundtrack of success, the amateur actresses' anticipation grows, although in a mostly good way.

It's time for make-up.
From the glare of dozens of lightbulbs surrounding their dressing mirror – this place naturally has all the props of a proper Theatre - the girls do their faces and practice their lines one last time. Mag stares mostly at Maria who keeps reassuring her and is able to make her Bff look flawless with no trace of former tears. When everyone is successfully transformed into their specific character, Helen takes over the pep talk.

Under their musical leaders' capable guidance the show gets off to a good start. The cast sails fairly smoothly over a few unimportant errors: one of the boys with a significant role forgets a line in the second act, and Mag's voice is shaky at the beginning of her first solo. By the end of the show, however, her singing is impeccable: airy tones dripping with expression and vocal ornamentations. The joint crescendo in the finale is goosebump-inducing.

Backstage, Maria soaks up the full power of it, listening with her whole being, tears streaming down her cheeks.

The audience seems satisfied and applauds for a good while. Some people even stand up, although it might be mostly parents. Someone shouts, "Bravo!" Maria has hardly noticed the crowd but now searches the auditorium for familiar faces. Oh, there's Christian, smiling while pulling at his red beard, looking surprisingly awake. He has helped with piano tutorials, she remembers. Right beside him, his gracious son is standing, clapping with a delighted face.

Maria's heart swells. He came!

The proud cast raises their joined hands in the air as they move to the edge of the stage and take a bow. Mag is glowing. What started out in the balance, ended a big success!

Eagerly, Maria scans the audience again.

There's no sign of Gregg.

~ Five ~

Summer solitaire

Jay's out the door before Maria has a chance to ask him what he meant.

Her blood begins to boil. How come he always does that? It's infuriating! She rises from the kitchen table, rushes into her bedroom and slams the door in a highly out-of-character way. The sound reverberates through silent space. Nobody else is home. No one notices her upset.

The story of her life.

Maria can't even call her Bff who's auditioning right about now. As far as she knows, Mag is counting on a life-changing occurrence this weekend: that she'll be discovered and chosen as Vanguard Villains' new backing singer and as such will be invited along on their upcoming summer tour. One of their regulars, Lori, is pregnant and soon has to stop touring. This afternoon, VIPs will be dropping by the recording studio: the band's big shot manager and some A & R people from that major label, they've signed a record deal with. Gregg has been putting a good word in for her in advance, he says.

Mag is positive she's on the brink of breaking into the music scene.

Since Mag is a minor, they wanted her parents to come, too, but as they are in the middle of what sounds like an acrimonious divorce, only the mother is going. Her daughter is, after all, only sixteen.

Other supporting characters, like best friends, are, on the other hand, not required at the meeting which takes place in another town.

Maggie's mother, Carol, is a super busy caterer in her mid-forties, literally juggling several plates at once. How much she sounds like Rick is uncanny and how little she looks like Mag, a mystery. "Oh, dad always says, I take after granny," Mag explained, once the subject came up. The only time Maria's met Carol, though, was at the spring concert when they celebrated backstage after the show. Mag's mom struck Maria as someone rather out-of-place among artists and creatives.

That night, she brought by a freshly made batch of chicken sandwiches, concerned if her youngest had eaten. The food was a hit and tasted great. It seems a bit unlikely, however, that this unpretentious, stressed woman could be of much help in landing contracts in showbiz...

Last week, Maria, in her most diplomatic way, and after receiving a: "Sure, if she would like me to," to the idea from Helen, suggested her city mama went with Mag instead or as well, but her idea got turned down. "Mom will do just fine. Besides, the more appraising eyes on me, the more nervous, I'll only get," Mag looked away, the loyal daughter.

Gobbling up Maria's thoughtful input while not following her counsel, as usual.

Jay made a comment about it, before heading out the door: "Uhm, don't take this the wrong way, but I feel like Maggie... uh, she's kinda using you, Maria, using you as a convenient prop. Like a real magpie, she seems pretty consumed with shiny objects." The words came out in his usual tentative way like always when something's at stake. And it stung, stung bad. Caught her off guard and left her speechless.

She can get so mad at him! Why on earth, doesn't he like Mag? It's so unlike him to be nasty.

Luckily, her new Bff hasn't noticed anything. She hardly ever mentions Jay.

Although once, at one of Rick's parties, they were chatting about boys, when Mag said something along the lines of how Maria's Jay looks quite cute, even if in a bit lame or undernourished way, not like the buff Gregg who makes an effort to stay fit. Maria, uncomfortable by the convo, explained that she's never thought of Jay that way. He's more of a kindred spirit or brother to her, twin even... She felt short for words. Then again, at that point, Mag was so wasted, she didn't really listen anymore.

Maria turns around on her bed and cast her red-rimmed eyes upon the ceiling. The pressure in her veins has lowered and the blood reached a tolerable temperature. Why does she always end up crying when cross, even if she, above any other emotion, feels abject anger? Always succumbing to tears makes her feel weak. She hates it!

Not that she would want to eliminate sorrow itself, could she. She wouldn't want to lose any color on the palette of emotions, merely balance the amount of each. While blue nuances can be beautiful, Maria would love to no longer have the darkest shade of blue as a somber backdrop underneath all other emotions, so often bleeding into them.

To paint one's future on a clean canvas seems only fair.

Her mind strays and old memories of earlier fears and anxieties come flooding in.

One by one, her childhood hideaways present themselves. Maria pictures her four-year-old self peeking through a peephole in the cloth from under the table at family gatherings. And later on, sitting up high in her private watchtower: the apple tree by the gable of their house, observing and coming to terms with the world, in particular its population... How often she had to steal a moment to herself in the restroom in elementary school. Or, how she, as a timid troubled tween, stayed inside her bedroom for days.

Despite its obvious downsides, solitary life is simple. Pure.

Why are people so complicated, so difficult to deal with? Even being around Jay can at times feel cumbersome. If not absorbed in a creative endeavor, he's the epitome of a human tuning fork: so super sensitive and emotionally perceptive that he notices and responds to everything. His face gives him away, he can't pretend. Not for very long, anyway. Sometimes, just sometimes, it can be a little tiring to handle such honesty, such a level of realness...

A ravenous craving for solitude, nearly as strong as any starvation for food, consumes Maria. Ahh, solitude: her good old reliable escape, best if surrounded by nothing but the peace and invigorating energies of nature; earthy smells of pine, grass and heather. To be in her element again, living by the natural rhythm of her autonomous heart.

How could she ever think, she could become some posh and popular city girl with cool friends and all? It's preposterous!

A paradox dawns on Maria. Who is she right now, then: the neglected one or the one left happily alone? No question, she is, most definitely, a part of the human race! Something melts inside her: the lump in her throat disappears and a chuckle softens her brow. She sits up with a sigh. Pondering how that pivotal audition's gonna turn out, she starts singing one of the songs they've practiced: her favorite. Maria's sadness dissolves like a sweetener in a cup of tea.

Singing is a natural mood-lifter, only she tends to forget because Mag is the talented one. The one with the bright future.

The phone rings, interrupting her flow.

It's Maggie. Exalted, she rambles on, hard to comprehend. It went well; or maybe not exactly as planned but still great, albeit in a slightly different direction. "This is gonna be my best summer EVER!" Mag close to cries. After the auditionee's settled down, Maria gets the whole story:

The manager, Mr. Blacksmith or Blackie as the boys call him, was, despite a crazy schedule, able to listen to Mag for a few songs. The experienced pro was dazzled by Mag's voice: how seamlessly she slides up and down the tonal scale without hiccups. He only seemed bummed by the fact that she's still so young: apparently, that's the real culprit. "I know you're hoping for representation, and we **are** interested but can't sign a contract with you until you're eighteen for it to be legal," he said, eying Mag's mom. "Yes, I realize," she sighed, "and it **is** flattering... Uh, I'm not certain if Maggie is mature enough for touring, and I, myself, know zip about the music business; perhaps better we wait..?" she raised her eyebrows.

"I was about to get a hissy fit!" Mag moans, Maria can literally hear her friend rolling her eyes through the receiver.

But, and here comes the silver lining, Gregg who was there, too, had a suggestion: what if, whenever the band's back in town this summer, Maggie drops by the studio? Then she could practice with them, gain some experience and a feel for the job. No pay as of yet, but great practice and no touring until old enough. Lori could show her the ropes, too, when she felt fit for it: a sort of informal internship?

"Super idea," Blackie was thrilled: " if it's alright with your big sis... er, I mean: your mother?" he winked and sent Maggie's mother a gallant smile. And it was. If only her daughter prioritizes school work until summer break and doesn't stay any later than ten in the evening: "Maggie needs her sleep."

A verbal agreement was made there and then. On a try-out basis and for Mag alone: what is expected to be Vanguard Villains' breakthrough album has now reached its finishing phase, and they don't want random people snooping around their quarters.

"We'll see how things go - after what I've heard today, I've got high hopes!" the manager ended the meeting, before rushing off to another one with another band.

In closing, Mag starts humming like always when chuffed, "Gregg actually does believe in me, you were right, homegirl!" Maria laughs, "Of course, he does. And not only him; we **all** do, Mag. Just don't forget what matters most is that **you** do."

The conversation proved to be the first in a long line of rambling phone calls from Maggie that summer. When school closes, she spends most of her time over at the studio. If the band isn't on the road, she'll catch a ride in Gregg's car: a shabby green Volkswagen Westfalia on the brink of replacement. And when they're touring, she takes the train, spending most of her parents' allowance on fare. Lori, heavier by the day, stops touring, but as she lives nearby, often visits the studio. A mentee is born.

The aspiring backing singer is all in: five foot five body and immeasurable soul!

Maria doesn't see much of her Bff but hears a lot: long daily reports carried through willing wavelengths. Lots of gossip about Lori, Gregg and the rest of the band and whoever else drops by the famous address. Real stars record there as well as a lot of semi-known singers and musicians.

Before fall, Maggie's got an impressive collection of autographs.

For Maria, it turns out a less memorable summer. Yet, living vicariously is familiar and effortless for her to adapt to. It feels safe and pleasant.

The season is abnormally hot, this year. Despite how unbearable the heat gets in the city with sweltering humid air and a burning pavement beneath flip-flops, she decides to cut her summer stay at Matter Island down to two weeks. A fortnight is enough somewhere you're beginning to feel out of place. Then she can travel light, too. She doesn't tell anyone beforehand, though.

One sure thing happens as soon as Maria sets foot on the island: right after "Sticky Waters" has been traversed, she slips into an old mold as easily as into a pair of old slippers. Super comfortable ones which feel that way because they're so worn. Whilst, first a blister, then sore toes and lastly bad abrasions reveal the shoes to be utterly outgrown. How they are, in fact, falling apart at the seams and unable to support your feet any longer; soles paper-thin, heels hanging out the rim.

Back in her parents' garden, sitting in the shade of the only elm tree spared by that disease all their other ones died from years ago, her mother asks about school.

Maria starts talking about how awesome the spring concert was. How being part of its production, even a very small part behind the scenes, is the single most satisfying experience she ever had. How it was such a success, receiving raving reviews, praising, among others, Maggie. And how Fairview made money enough for setting up an even bigger production next year. Maria's last sentence has her mother react. For a second, she stares dumbfounded at her daughter as if she was a stranger. Mom seems a little uncomfortable, "City folks will pay good money to watch high school kids do a school play...?" Maria nods. "Well, now I never!" baffled, mom wipes her forehead with a handkerchief, not knowing what to say.

Maria tries to share about her life, tries to accommodate her mother's curiosity which sometimes feels closer to interrogation. Her answers are often received with a hint of suspicion, her mom's face, at times, displays ill-concealed disbelief. Yet this is familiar. Harder is sharing subjects close to her heart: which philosophical ponderings occupy her mind or which recent personal dots she's discovered and connected into insights. Her parents are humble yet proud villagers and anything sounding too abstract, artsy or hoity-toity, as Elsie from the fish factory once called it, is deemed irrelevant. They have no interest in or need for it, and what's more, lack the language.

"Maybe you'll soon be invited to do an interview for the morning show on telly? Shouldn't you do something about those tousled curls of yours, then? There must be plenty of top-notch hairdressers in the city... and maybe wear a longer skirt, huh?" mom pulls playfully at one of the pleats in her daughter's summer skirt. Maria puts her left leg across the right one, safely out of reach. Examining Maria upon arriving has become a ritual to break the ice caused by their current distance. Out of sheer interest for her well-being, according to mom, besides design, of course. Maria's mother always emphasizes how much she admires Helen's fashion eye. It might be partly true, but a certain pretense is hard to miss. With a light, disarming smile, the summer-clad girl picks her brain for other topics.

How come, seconds into chatting with mom, Maria feels like a suspicious character, her anxiety and insecurity amplified? It never happens with Helen or Margaret...

It's safest to shift back to Maggie's adventures, like the great reviews she received for her singing in the spring show and now, rehearsing at a famous studio. Thank god for Mag's good fortune. It's Maria's only claim to fame and a handy diversion from her own lack of such.

Down at the harbor, the cruise ship construction has come to an unexpected halt, to the villagers' great discontent. The ships should already be cruising the balmy waters surrounding the island; the weather's perfect for it. The final papers of permit are, however, for inexplicable reasons delayed. And Bill and Jack's hands are tied until receiving these. The tourists have to stay patiently on shore and find other means of amusement.

The constant ding-donging of the Mini Market's doorbell next door attests that their neighbor's ice cream and cheap plastic beach toys are highly spoken for. On Tuesday, Maria heads over there to say hi to Stella, who's busy filling goods on shelves at her dad's store. Her old friend is wearing a black sleeveless t-shirt and dungarees. The chubby cheeks have grown chubbier. She seems moody, doesn't chuckle constantly like she used to. The sun's made the freckles on Stella's nose reproduce and be more noticeable than ever, but besides that, her natural charm is hiding well.

The resemblance to Maggie has diminished considerably.

Sliding back into her former self, Maria gets insecure. She barely manages to ask how Stella's summer has been? From a squatting position next to the bottom shelf, Stella gazes dull-eyed up at Maria for a moment, then her face softens and she sighs, "If you really want to know, I've been stuck in town. Dad's used like a gazillion of money on expanding the store which means no vacation for us, at least this year. Instead of hired help, I have to step in until the loan's paid out. Won't take long, he's promised. I can't wait!" a flash of the good old headstrong Stella resurfaces. She gets up and rests her hands in the trouser pockets, inhaling deeply.

Woes, eager to be shared, are visibly stirred below Stella's frown. Maria regrets going here: to be a soft landing place for unloading the trials and tribulations of one friend at a time will suffice. After expressing a few clunky words of compassion, she hastily leaves and doesn't come back. Five minutes later, Maggie calls. Listening to her new Bff retell her love interest's funny or clever remarks and cheering her on removes the remnants of guilt regarding the old one.

Her fellow city girl's exploits are, to be honest, way cooler...

For once, Maria's father has vacation while she's back. The heat makes him edgy. Instead of relaxing, he gets restless, wandering about the house and garden. The high temperatures make it impossible to work outside, though. Idleness is sensible.

Her last week on the island comes with a welcome increase in wind and the heat gets bearable. Dad and John drive off in the station car to go fly-fishing: that's their new bonding hobby. Maria's father, besides, got a new dinghy last year and when weather permits spends hours fishing just like when he was a kid.

Peace settles upon the house, interrupted only by the frequent calls from Mag.

Her Bff's current rubbing shoulders with celebrities ends up a continued soap series with Maria providing the next episode after each phone call. Her mother is in awe of anyone who appears on stage, above all, on screen, though. People she knows from her favorite TV shows are bordering on buddies: admired, fortunate, if faraway friends. How they got there she sees as being likely in-born: some rare and blessed boon. Fame is a heaven-sent gift for a talented few.

After surfing the channels, they stumble upon a popular show back from Maria's early childhood, and soon they're both enjoying themselves, chatting about good old times. "As a toddler, you were such a curious and happy little girl with a smile that brightened my cloudy days. Later, you always seemed to be lost in a book or your own thoughts," her mother's face is soft and her eyes pre-sent. Tugs at Maria's heartstrings; if only mom was like this more often.

When the TV isn't on, mom will try to persuade Maria to play cards with her by the garden table, but her daughter's pretty hopeless at these games. It doesn't interest her. After a while, mom sighs as deeply as only a mother can and takes to do a deck of solitaire: a game she often plays.

One of the last days, the topic of conversation, unavoidably, re-verts to her parents' marital problems. It's not the first time the reluctant young girl, in a heavy-hearted role reversal, tries to act as her mother's counselor. Wasted words, since she's seeking con-solation and doesn't really listen to her child, anyway. Mom wants momentary relief, not an excavation to find the root cause or any solution. Maria's worked that much out, by now...

Her dad grumbles a bit when Maria asks him about driving her back to the city earlier than expected. "Okay then, if you'll catch the train halfway," he finally nods. "Send Helen my love!" her mother yells in parting, even if the two women ever since Maria's move to the city have become less close. Maybe her father's bad mouth?

Whatever the reason, the gap is growing; impossible not to notice. A saddening fact that often worries their daughter.

After a quiet, sweaty car ride and noisy ditto by train, Maria and her light baggage arrive in the drowsy city, where the heat seems to have slowed down the pace of life.

Jay and his family, except big sister Lisa who's traveling, are still summering at The Meadow Muse. No Spot, wagging his tail and whole body, comes rushing over to greet her as soon as the front door opens. Maria plonks, first the bag then herself, down on one of the soft sofas. The living room is strangely still, only dust particles whirl in the rays of the late afternoon sun.

Matter Island living and big city living is like living in, not merely different places but on different planets. Transitioning from one to the other, it takes hours to acclimate.

Letting her shoulders drop, Maria exhales, relieved about having the place to herself.

Relieved she's got time and space for digesting her latest island visit.

~ Six ~

Fall is nearing

School begins again for the first of their senior years.

At Fairview, grades are, to be in alignment with the institution's visionary spirit, given in a less prescribed and more creative way, using different parameters than most high schools use. Just like their class periods and timetable, the syllabus is a bit more fluid. Even so; in the last two years of their education they **will** be evaluated and most of the students aim for and need to get good grades for their college application. Girls and boys alike contemplate, religiously, choosing the perfect mayor. If someone asks Maria, however, she'll be waffling, fast diverting the conversation in another direction.

Nowhere more than here, do the pupils' background differences come clear.

When it happens to cross Maria's mind, and she does her best not to let it, a sense of impending doom will creep in. What next?

Jay has his choir work and band plans, besides occasionally stepping in, tutoring piano instead of his dad, if he for some reason can't. It's starting to earn him a little money. Maggie's got total tunnel vision, too. Considering how a love of music and singing is the common denominator for her two closest friends, it's so odd that they don't see eye to eye; don't vibe at all.

Not only Mag and Jay; everybody in class has exciting plans, it seems. Everybody but her. When airing her concerns to Margaret, the trusted teacher reassures her there's plenty of time to figure things out. Maria **is** one year younger than the rest and there's still a way to go before graduation. No rush.

Mag, on the other hand, seems less and less concerned about school. When they're
handed this year's reading list, she hardly deigns it a second glance. Unlike Maria, analyzing paragraphs or meticulously dissecting sentences down to single words to extract a metaphorical or potentially profound point, doesn't make her tick.

She's not even that interested in lyrics; it's singing that gratifies. The applause, also.

"What am I doing here, I belong with my music peeps!" Maggie will exclaim, whether it's writing an essay, assigning literary criticism to a contemporary piece or one of the classics, or analyzing a poem by Keates has her pulling out her hair. "Ah, never mind, because if so **we** wouldn't be together: I absolutely need my bestie by my side!" she'll laugh, leaning against Maria whose heart melts anytime Mag shows affection.

Not knowing why, the, possibly sidetracked, songbird's bestie is starting to feel a bit queasy as well.

Maggie's father is a writer/journalist working for a tabloid paper. He was the one thinking she'd be better off choosing creative writing, also since singing lessons are obligatory for every wing at Fairview: a unifying thread that binds them all together.

Talented or not; one could get the idea that he's not so keen on his daughter heading down a career path in music...

Likely striving to accommodate her dad's wants and wishes has more to do with it, but the more Maggie complains, the more her bestie feels somehow responsible for her friend's growing sense of being misplaced. How could she be that, when the two of them are so alike? She glances at Mag's outfit: the skimpy skirt and the make-up; a layer seemingly getting thicker by the day. None of the other girls in class dress quite so poppish, nor does she. For every-day use, Maria only wears a bit around the eyes; more than that and her eczema flares up.

Gee, maybe it's true: isn't Mag starting to stick out like a sore thumb? Maria's heart breaks for her Bff who moves ahead as before, blissfully indifferent to such worries.

Maria makes subtle attempts at sparking Mag's interest in the varied literary field, trying to convince her of its artistic advantages and intrinsic rewards. Maggie doesn't have Maria's literary sensibilities, though.

Being graciously granted a free pass to Vanguard Villains' inner circle is an honor Maggie takes great pride in. In fact, it's **so** important to her that she even declines when offered the leading role in the school's spring musical: a playful rendition with a healthy dose of feminism and the promising title "A Fair View on a Lady".

"I would rather use all of my spare time on practicing with the band," she reasons, after a brief deliberation. Maria doesn't get her bestie's choice, but Mag won't budge.

No one asks Maria if she'll help out again. Disappointed, she decides to skip the show altogether, too. Without Mag, what's the point?

It's only natural that the ambitious amateur does what she can to pull her Bff along into her all-consuming passion project: to secure herself a spot on the music scene. Maria's not much of a warrior: the energetic tug of war tends to tip in Mag's favor.

In early fall, a summery Saturday in September, Vanguard Villains debut album "Break Down the Bars" finally gets released after successfully releasing its lead single, the title track, and after months of marketing efforts to generate maximum interest.

Mr. Blacksmith encourages Mag to invite two of her friends to the release party at the legendary venue "Star Gate" close to the studio. Rick and Maria are the lucky chosen ones to join her, the band, their crew, manager and several music journalists, besides a crowd of famous, or at least famouish, folks attending this super hot event.

When hearing of it, Maria's mother is impressed, and with Rick present there as well, getting permission isn't a major issue. Maggie's father is, besides, one of the invited from the press, even if they're not exactly going together. "Just remember temperance with the beverages, of course, and to watch out for frisky young men. Oh, and I need to see photos; you better shoot a whole bunch!" mom orders.

Maria promises and so is, fairly easily, let off the hook.

The big release

The two besties, with Rick tagging along, arrive at the venue early.

Mag got her backstage pass, so they all discretely slip in the back door, escaping adoring fans standing in line at the front: squealing young girls along with some quieter boys. Both groups are clearly prepared to get inside, one way or another.

Maggie looks dazzling in a skimpy black dress full of sequins. With her make-up on sun-kissed skin, big sunglasses and blond hair pulled elegantly back in a bun, she looks five years older. The girl beside her is wearing a little less make-up and sporting a pigeon blue silk dress in Helen's feminine design. Tonight, Maria feels like a real woman, too, proud to be part of this glitz and glam.

They can hear the band do sound checks on stage. The psyched girls' eyes meet and both smile excitedly. Maria's pulse rises.

The three of them find their way to the empty, except for busy waiters, lobby and the girls grab a fancy, poisonous-looking lime-green cocktail from one of several gold trays on pedestals. Huge band-posters are up everywhere. The four guys flash their white teeth at people from every corner of the room: Gregg winks at the camera, his thick, dark eyebrows curled into an expression of cunning coolness.

Rick complains he would rather have a beer and heads out to find one, leaving the euphoric girls behind, not protesting his departure.

Girlishly giggling, they find themselves a perfect spot with a good view toward the entrance where guests are starting to pour in. With deft fingers, Maggie shoves the sunglasses up on her head. They're huge and hiding her baby blues behind them has become an integral part of Mag since the audition where Gregg complimented her on her cool style.

Maria's made a habit of simply hiding hers behind her long bangs.

Last night, she revealed to her bestie how boggling bad at banter she has always been. Put on the spot, she can never come up with anything clever to say. Her mind betrays her and only delivers the most insipid drivel: it never fails! Maria made Mag promise to, smoothly, interrupt the conversation if she catches her getting flustered chatting to someone significant.

Laughing, they even invented a secret hand sign she could use.

Sipping at their drinks, the girls take turns stretching necks, eager to get a glimpse of celebrities or maybe a gorgeous model. Mag proudly points out some musicians she knows from the studio: the coolest ones. Two of the rare, royal breed walk right by!

People from the press and a few paparazzi start showing up. Mag goes quiet.

The shine of the setting sun briefly vanishes, as one of the city's prominent reporters' substantial pondus takes up most of the doorway. Right at his heels, he's got a slender, sleepy-looking stubbled guy with a huge camera hanging around his neck. A subtle grey comes over the pretty blonde's face. Her posture collapses slightly and the beam in her eyes dulls.

Maggie's father has entered the building.

To Maria the man's merely a name, occasionally photo, inside slick tabloid magazines, pointed out by her friend. But she easily recognizes the square proportioned physique, similar to Rick's was it more toned. He's got a plumpish face with the complexion of brie cheese, garnished by a mustache and freshly colored brown hair, thinning at the top. No playful joy bubbles beneath the surface here, though; the impression of Mag's dad is one of laser-focused professionalism. His movements are casual, almost lazy. The aqua blue eyes, though, the only outward trait resembling his daughter, are sharp and fast as they scan the entire lobby.

"Damn, didn't think, they would let the press in through the front door..." Mag bites her lip, diving down behind a tall fella standing next to their tray table, but too late: her father has seen her. He stops in his tracks, hesitates, then steers toward them.

"What the hell, Maggie, I almost didn't recognize you, there," his voice is calm with a guttural rasp. He sounds like someone who, heavily exposed to everything life brings, no longer gets surprised. The middle-aged man seems to assess the pros and cons of his daughter's new look. His face is, however, devoid of expression and doesn't give away any conclusion.

Through twitchy eyes, Maria notices a stain on his grey shirt which, by the way, could use some ironing. Perturbed, she gazes at her shoes as her stomach drops. Uh-oh, are they in trouble?

"I did tell you, I was invited, dad! Rick is here somewhere, too, and this is Maria: the girl I've been telling you about," Mag eagerly diverts her father's attention to her Bff. Maria tentatively lifts her eyes and sends the reporter a forced, dry-mouthed, smile.

Maggie's dad ignores her, "You already know my view on these types of parties, it gets crazy later on. You better go home in a few hours, okay? I'll get Rick to drop you off at his place." The grey-ness subsides and Mag's face turns starkly red against her blond hair. She nods, tears glistening beneath downcast eyelids. Staying silent, she fast flips her sunglasses back on.

The father takes a glance at the unassuming, artless girl next to his daughter:

"Who's Maria again?"

The tabloid newshound's photographer shows up behind him: "Come on, Joe! We better get in there soon if we want a decent spot," he impatiently pats him on the shoulder. Mag's dad nods and narrow-eyed leans in toward his daughter: " Meet me outside by the back entrance right after the band Q&A – be ready!" Then he is gone.

The evening is ruined.

Despite Maria acting anxiously silly and cracking up about a celebrity lady wearing a frog that looks like her grandma's velvet curtains, Mag is inconsolable. Defeated, they drink up. Mag snatches herself another one, and then they follow the crowd to the stage to join a merry mix of famous colleagues or peers in pop, devoted fans and more level-headed, people of the press. The crowd is divided and guided into three areas: VIPs and people from the band's innermost circles chilling on the balcony, fans stand-ing front stage on the floor and the music press placed at a side lounge.

Mag keeps peeking at the balcony, yet to become part of that golden entourage...

Heat rises in the room, and at 9pm sharp, the band, minus backing singers, comes storming in and the dishy Marcus grabs the mic without further ado. The whole audience screams in delight except the dejected teenage girl in black and her faithful confidante in blue. The only thing that, at least momentarily, restores Mag's party mood, is when Gregg, in a tank-top revealing more tattoos on flexed muscles and standing at the edge of the stage, aims his crooked smile as well as his shiny Fender bass in her direction.

The young performer's gesture breaks the spell.

Letting out a girly cry, Maggie's face opens up in a wide, worshipping grin, and the bass player moves on to spoil other ravenous individuals of the female kind. He and the little jet engine of a lead singer take turns in captivating a select subdivision of the audience. Even if Maria isn't graced with special attention, she is, like everybody else, sucked into the hard-and-fast rhythm of their upbeat dance tunes; her feet unable to stand still. After the sixth song, her head is spinning, though, and when their set ends after song number seven, she is relieved.

It's time for band Q&A: the press is waiting.

Strong roadies swiftly remove the band's gear from the stage to replace it with a long table and comfortable chairs. Still sweaty, the four band members stroll on stage to sit down, appearing relatively nonchalant about the hullabaloo. Blackie is standing by in the wings, almost invisibly.

The fans, except for a couple of diehard ones who've won the opportunity to ask the band a question, are herded to the side as the press takes over. A lot of blitzing ensues. Maggie is transfixed by what happens on stage, but it reminds Maria to shoot some photos herself. Sadly, she's too shy to aim her camera at any of the close-by celebrities. Overwhelmed and star-struck, her movements are clumsily stiff: most of the pictures turn out blurry or off-kilter. She drops it.

What's to come, they're both unprepared for.

It starts out entertaining yet well-mannered. Three lucky fan-girls are up first and stuttering and blushing ask Marcus rather personal questions which he answers with some tongue-in-cheek one-liners. Everybody laughs. The room is boiling, now. The people of the press swoops in. A journalist from a respected music magazine wants to know about their background and the inspiration behind the new album and Gregg speaks briefly about their main influences and the music in technical terms. A tipsy fan interrupts this sudden seriousness, "Marry me!" The boys in the band smirk, wiping sweat off their faces or having a sip of sparkling water. People laugh again.

Maggie's dad is up next.

"First of all: congratulations. For a debuting band, you guys are certainly turning some heads," neither the reporter's face nor voice reveal any ill intent. The boys thank him.

Maria sends Mag a heartening smile which is reciprocated; the shine in her friend's eyes has returned.

"One can't help but wonder, though, if this rapid, almost overnight, success is a well-deserved achievement for true talent and musicianship or more of a lucrative hoax set up by greedy money men behind the scenes. It wouldn't be the first time, but if that's the case or not, I shan't be the judge of." Loud booing from the rest of the audience. The photographer beside Mag's father, slides unaffected around, taking photos from different angles.

Maria tenses up. Her Bff's eyes are huge and bluer than ever. Her mouth opens.

Gregg sits up straight in his chair. Even from a distance, they can see his jaws tighten. With a jolt, Mag starts shoving people aside to move closer to the stage. Maria, the little lemming, follows her with a heart pounding ever harder.

"This album is made by Vanguard Villains' combined talents and hard work with the finishing touch of our professional producer, of course. What are you insinuating?"

Gregg leans in over the table with an intense stare.
"Just a general observation, no offense. All right, we'll lay that one to rest for now... I am, besides, more concerned about some rumors circulating of underaged girls being served alcohol – and god knows what else – backstage after your concerts."

"You don't have to answer that, Gregg!" Blackie comes out of the shadows, "the band will, of course, only answer relevant questions. Keep the tone, please: these fine young men certainly don't deserve any slandering or a smear campaign! Let's have the next one, and let me remind you again to focus on the music."

The audience applauds and hollers. Mag's dad lets go of the mic. With a head shake, he slowly steps back and takes a seat.

"Who let that tabloid bully in here!" a young fangirl in front of them yells heatedly.

In the meantime, it has dawned on Maria, caught in her hooked bestie's slipstream, how utterly in over her head she is in all of this. For a second, her panicky eyes search for an exit sign, but with a wall of Villains, as hardcore fans religiously call themselves, surrounding her, she has to give up and prepare to play her familiar role.

Once again, she lets her eyes land on Maggie who has hers fixated on Gregg.

When Blackie appears, midway through the crowd, Mag changes her mind as well as direction. Instead, she starts pushing her way to a rope that marks the backstage area. Finally, she stops to turn around and talk to her Bff, not doubting she is behind her.

And, indeed, Maria is.

"I knew dad might do something rotten, he's that mad!" Maggie's body shivers with agitation, "he is ruining my life; this treachery, I will **never** forgive him for," her voice chokes up. Maria gets chest pains, "So sorry, Mag. Maybe he wants to protect you...?" sobering fast, she nervously picks her brain to find mitigating aspects to his deed.

"Fuff, that would be a first then... He only cares about himself: his shoddy high profile job and that conniving minx he's hooked up with!" Mag jumps the rope sideways like a little kid which her tight dress won't allow. Instead, she trips and falls on the floor, hurting her ankle. Out of the blue, her face crumbles.

The backstage lounge is empty. Using Maria as a crutch, Mag limps, sobbing loudly, over to a sofa arrangement meant for performers. The teen girl now cries so hard, she close to hyperventilates. On the coffee table are two mugs with a splash of coffee, sodas, some emptied cocktail glasses and a nearly half-full bottle of rum. As soon as safely seated, Maggie takes a swig of the liquor.

Overpowering powerlessness befalls her, now stone cold sober, Bff.

Choked, Maria watches Maggie drink the rest of the bottle; still bawling at first then slowly settling down. Despite the balmy September evening, she's chilled to the bone. Tonight, Claire doesn't materialize. In this darkness, she's inadequately alone.

For the first time ever, no words are spoken between them. Maggie stares stiffly into space with a pained expression, sniffling and absently rubbing her ankle from time to time. She, at least, doesn't seem to be cold.

Minutes pass. Then the sound of thunderous applause, followed by Blackie saying thank you to the press and declaring the bar open. "Let's get this party started, folks!" Loud music thumps through the building, the floor vibrates below their feet.

Maggie sends Maria an absent glance. She puts down the emptied bottle and gets on her feet, tryingly resting half of her body weight on the left leg. "It's okay now," she says, pacing back and forth. Only a slightly slouching gait reveals the compromised state. Maria wakes up from her own, "Are you sure you're okay...?" Not meeting her eyes, Mag nods, "Let's go."

Maria leads the way to the exit, slightly ahead of her injured soul sister.

~ S e v e n ~

Haphazard hayseeds

"Hey, pass the glue stick - can't get anything done when you hog it like that!" Maggie stretches a limp-looking hand toward Maria.

The teenage girl sounds perky as usual, but unlike the sunrays that peek through the arched windows of the classroom as welcome messengers of spring, Maggie's sunny disposition is noticeably lacking today. She's listless, seems bored. Her current lifestyle is starting to show. Dark circles under the eyes enhance a sickly pale complexion even a heavy layer of make-up can't hide. Mag's blue soul ponds themselves have turned as grey and dull as a stagnant ocean on an overcast day in January.

When their eyes meet, Maria scarcely recognizes her.

Earlier, this Monday morning, Mag told her that she wasn't feeling well and might leave early. Her best friend, of course, showed empathy, but this is honestly not the first time it happens; Mag has been cutting class an awful lot, lately. Hangover again?

With a complaisant little laugh, Maria hands the glue stick to her poorly friend.

Maggie, as suspected, leaves before noon after a brief encounter with Margaret. Their teacher stares concerned at her pale pupil for a moment then tenderly strokes her arm and wishes a speedy recovery. Afterward, her eyes search to find Maria's and when they meet, the teen smiles reassuringly with a shrug and a what-can-I-say expression on her face. Margaret shakes her head, hesitantly moving on to someone else in need of assistance.

As opposed to Maria's outward demeanor; her heart sinks like a free-falling skydiver. It's getting ever more obvious that she'll end up finishing their co-creative project alone. Again!

The last time was during the first term project in the middle of 1st semester. In their senior years, they have two major ones, each spanning three weeks. The first one in October was defined from the offset while the second one landing on their desks came with limitless artistic license. It was a highly anticipated moment.

Back in autumn, they still were granted a lot of liberty, though. It turned out, they had to do a modern re-telling of one of the classic fairy tales: "The Little Match Girl". Seeing it, Maria's heart skipped a beat out of pure joy. Her childhood favorite!

Mag was maybe a little less excited, but everything started out fine. They decided on writing a spin-off manuscript complemented by a mix of poetry and photo collages. "Haphazard Hayseeds or Country Girls Catch Fire in the City: A Modern-day Tale in Words & Imagery": the long title was Maggie's cut-to-the-chase wording, causing quite a few laughs. The description undeniably fits, even if a connection to the classic wasn't quite clear yet...

Little did Maria know that coming up with the wordy title would end up Mag's only contribution, but from there on her bestie's creative well apparently ran dry and their collaboration went downhill fast.

It was once again unusually hot, a period of Indian Summer. On school days, Mag wouldn't show up as promised to work on their project but always had something more important going on. At weekends, she would travel home to see her mother who, all of a sudden, needed her help. While away, Mag phoned all the time, though, talking incessantly about Gregg and how everything's about to come together for her. As visiting the studio is no longer off-limits for outsiders, she would fervidly try to persuade her Bff, often succeeding in the end, to hang out there, waiting around for Mag to finish her singing practice or just chatting to other people at the studio.

Last fall, Maggie's favorite fellow and his homies really took off, despite that minor scandal at the release party which, in fact, conversely propelled their rise to stardom. Her critical father's claim on something being iffy didn't have the intended effect.

Thus distracted, Maggie's disappearing acts caused Maria several late nights of hard work to meet the term project deadline. At the last minute and in a state of panic, she picked up the pieces of the stranded script or rather conjured up and assembled brand new ones. With help from Jay, the necessitated night owl managed to put something decent together. Or rather half-decent, she sensed, sad that the imagined profound and layered modern version of the treasured tale never came to be.

Instead, the storyline was all over the place, the poetry pretty plain.

Even if Maria afterward felt like Margaret looked kinda funny at her, she pretended everything was fine. Her teacher said nothing, but the project came back with a C on it, underlinings in red and additional commentary. Apparently, Maria hadn't fully grasped the heart of the story.

Margaret must be so disappointed in the two of them but especially in Maria who loves fairy tales and normally excels at excavating its core message.

The current assignment of their own choosing began at the end of March. No one questioned if the Dotty Duo would join forces once more. And while everybody else in class was far above the moon, a sense of unease slowly grew in Maria.

"Creative freedom and contemporary art is much more **my** style," Mag stared at the project description over Maria's shoulder, "that dusty old tale was a drag, impossible to be inspired by. Gregg also thought it was a joke; so passée." Maria nodded, shoving a sting of discomfort to the side. The paper on her desk read only one line, in all caps:

"ART PROJECT WITH FULL ARTISTIC LICENSE – BE WILDLY CRE-ATIVE!".

From the get-go, they've been brimming with ideas, jotting the juiciest ones down, eager to dive into their project, just like Maria thought they were last semester. Yeah, in the beginning, they both seem inspired and fired up. Then something changes...

Lately, the supposed bedrock beneath their friendship has started cracking open in earth-shaking jerks, destabilizing her newfound steadiness of foot.

As soon as the start of April, Maria saw the other side of Maggie.

A dependable co-creative

Throughout winter, the girls' conversations got increasingly one-sided.

These days, Mag usually dives straight into complaining about her life in general and obsessing over her new flame in particular. Gregg is a hot-blooded young man, fairly susceptible to what he considers essential female assets. A small detail clear to Maria from the first time she met him.

Alas, her Bff is slipping away from her to mix with the in-crowd around Gregg; hanging about, drinking or throwing spontaneous parties after their gigs and stuff.

The lead singer, Marcus, is the youngest in the band, barely nineteen and an outgoing, speed-talking chap with sparkly hazel eyes and a long but well-groomed, stylish dark-blond quiff. Marcus likes to pull the others' legs whenever and wherever he gets a chance. Grinning, he'll call people "half brains" if they make mistakes or do anything remotely foolish. Marcus is never serious for long; their audience is always entertained in between songs. All the teenage girls swoon over him.

Maggie's sure he is the perfect guy for Maria due to the front-man status, his age and the fact that he isn't terribly tall. Three good reasons, she claims and makes suggestive hints whenever he's around. The crux of the matter, though, is how perfect it'll be for the four of them to go on double dates, then: herself & Gregg and Maria & Marcus. Generally being a little tipsy only adds to Maggie's uncalled-for match-making.

Secretly, Maria finds Marcus childish and obnoxious.

Sure, she's had a crush on him, fantasizing about being his chosen one like many other teenage girls. Daydreaming, she'd picture herself tenderly running her fingers through that soft-looking hair of his. But while Marcus is easy on the eyes, the same can't be said for sensitive ears... with his bratty behavior, her initial interest fades each time she meets the chap. Once, he aimed his flighty attention at Maria, wise-cracking a few fast words that went straight over her head in her shy awkwardness. When she didn't respond, he held a hand coyly to his lips, "Oops, guess it's true, then: you **do** suck at banter!" She cringed and felt blue. It must've slipped Mag's tongue.

Maria has a sneaking suspicion of being way too uncool for that crowd.

At first, she went along, but something about these young men, their raucous laughter and the witty, roistering way they talk make Maria's old twitchiness rear its ugly head. Appearance is everything, the music is way too loud, and she often ends up drinking too much, feeling awful the next day: headachy, nauseous, her ears ringing. Except for that Christmas incident a while ago, Mag now gulps the booze down, seemingly without repercussions, while Maria's starting to feel sick from the mere smell of beer. The last several times, Maria's made excuses for not going, despite Mag's complaints, despite how "Goddamn lucky a couple of high school kids are to be included," as her Bff, the present party girl, insists.

At this point, if Maria drinks at all, she does it to dampen an acute self-consciousness. Drinking will produce a needed buffer when she's around all that tumultuous teenage intensity, be it animation, agitation or angst.

After Gregg's arrival on the scene, Maria's soon-to-be seventeen bosom friend has slowly become more spirituous than spirited. Maggie seems deaf and blind to all else; any previous sensitivity to Maria's feelings is as good as gone. Those wonderfully wild ideas which used to pop and multiply like corns in a popcorn machine from the lively neurons of their minds get rerouted since Mag's focus is directed into a tunnel named Gregg. A downward spiraling one with no light at the end, Maria fears.

Maria's guts are in a knot, she fights an urge to leave early, too.

All previous sparks of inspiration have fizzled and died. With leaden arms, she glues random photos on here and there. Maybe she should talk to Margaret about it? Or maybe have a chat with Helen or Jay? On the other hand, if Jay were let in on this, he would perhaps pique himself on his hunch being correct...? Nope, she doesn't feel like giving him that satisfaction after he's sorta left her out in the cold, lately. Also, she shouldn't go behind Maggie's back; she would get real mad at Maria if she did.

She is nothing, if not loyal!

Quandarella swallows a lump and clenches her jaw. A headache's underway, and she discretely rubs her temples. Spring hasn't even registered in Maria. All her energy is sucked into straddling working hard on their creative project, pretty much alone, and keeping Mag in good spirits. Uplifting or humoring her bestie has become the new normal and her affection is slowly fading. She's becoming quieter, while the source of it all notices nothing and just goes on and on.

Maria doesn't sleep well. At night time, she tosses and turns, endlessly running the situation through her mind, worrying about Maggie. Searching for solutions. Her dreams are filled with pushing her way through raging snowstorms, exhausted, snow-blind and lost. It wouldn't surprise her if Mr. Freeze; that bloodless and bony specter from her girlhood nightmares is about to enter these dreary dreamscapes.

When she wakes in the morning, reality isn't much warmer. How can Maggie not see, that she's stepping on the edge of quicksand? That she deserves better than Gregg; how he isn't trustworthy? Or is Maria imagining things, exaggerating? Except for this, they usually experience situations the same way, don't they? They're of one mind about most things, aren't they? She hardly knows left from right, anymore...

After everything's said and done, only they know what it's like for a small-town kid to be cast among privileged children of the fortunate, Maggie and her brother agree. In reality, Maggie only got enrolled at Fairview because of a scholarship and Maria has been lucky enough to have close to free housing and a hostess who is on the school-board committee, Rick likes to remind them.

"Gregg and the other guys in Vanguard Villains are street smart. While I'm sure they're nice enough and all, don't be mistaken: those spoiled rich kids and highfalutin teachers at your school know nothing about the struggles of regular people," Rick lectured during Maria's last visit, arms crossed over his manly chest. Maggie nodded and grinning impersonated "The String

Bean": no doubt the most flamboyant teacher at school and an esteemed bellwether from the music wing. The target is a very tall and very tender character with an androgynous appearance, hair like a frizzy grey mic, colorful clothes and mannerism.

Maria laughed, too, and took a swig of her beer. In fact, she really likes the dear old dude but didn't say. Soon after, her belly contracted in burning spasms. Her tummy is acting up so often, lately, it's ridiculous!

Maria hasn't told her mom about this, but she mentioned it to Helen the other day. In a diverting way, though, touching on Rick and Maggie's appetite for fast food. "Aha! Too much pizza, chips and soft drinks; too little porridge, veggies and herbal tea, I suspect," Helen grinned, "My advice is to not wait too long between meals: if you're too hungry, you tend to not question the quality of food but will grab whatever junk is easily available. Looks like you'll have to sway them in a healthier direction, sweetie."

"Oh, **I**, of course, hardly touch any junk," Maria joked, "yeah, I guess you're right..." She didn't feel like spoiling that lightheartedness between them she enjoys so much, by spilling the beans completely.

Keeping what's essential under wraps is a hard-dying habit.

~ Eight ~

Long shadows of a winter past

"For Pete's sake, Maria, don't be so selfish! I thought, best friends were supposed to always be there for one another? Well, suit yourself, then!"

Maggie spits the words out with a voice shifting fast from accusatory and shrill to deeply vulnerable. Her cheeks are blushing and her big blue eyes briefly pierce Maria's before welling up with water. She bites her dusty pink lower lip and looks down, turning her back. The dark grey suede across the shoulders of her leather jacket shivers.

Maria bursts into tears. "I'm sorry, Maggie, it came out all wrong: I didn't mean it like that – please don't cry!" she pulls beggingly at one of her friend's fringed sleeves.

The door to the girls' restroom flings opens, as a couple of chatty seniors of Indian origin come in. The young women, wearing beautiful saris, hardly deign the dramatic scene a glance before dropping their school bags on the ground by the sink. Staring at each other more than into the mirror, they with swift fingers adjust or re-arrange the other one's long, shiny hair into elegant hairdos. Still chatting eagerly in their mother tongue, they enter two neighboring toilet booths.

Mag gives Maria the side-eye before sliding her sunglasses back on and rushing out the door, leaving her Bff dumb and guilt-stricken behind.

Oh, no, this wasn't supposed to happen: this is exactly what she's been trying to avoid for weeks!

Maria stares at the restroom door. Her feet are made of concrete, a part of the cold floor. She couldn't chase after Maggie if she wanted to. Maybe, she'll come back? Then Maria can explain herself better; choose other, better – kinder words. Minutes pass and only the two Indian girls approach and only to meticulously wash hands. Their conversation continues throughout the seance and they leave, still inhabiting a harmonious, private bubble of their own, galvanized against outside intrusion. An enviable one.

After they're gone, Maria's paralysis slowly subsides, and she slumps down on the wooden bench against the back wall, shivering.

School's out for today, and it's Wednesday before Easter. There's a flicker of light in that. Maggie has planned to go traveling with Gregg's band and their roadies. The band's hired to play some gigs down south and will be catching a plane tomorrow for an Easter tour to be back Monday. It's a tour involving advantageous interviews and photoshoots, plus posing to be on the next cover of a high-profile music magazine. Apparently, Gregg invited her and Maggie was, of course, dying to jump on board, "We can't turn down such an amazing adventure - I say, we do it!"

The whole cause of their row is that Maria doesn't want to join them. Rick, the main parental figure in Maggie's life as of late, is needed at his clerk job downtown on Easter Saturday and so can't go. He made one objection about the matter, saying his sister can go if only Maria does, too. It's just safer for two girls to stick together.

Every cell in Maria's body opposes it, and her mind's in overdrive to rationalize why.

She has until tomorrow to decide what to do next, and if she sticks with her intuition, the holidays to find the right words. What did she even say now? Maria can barely recall. An impermeable haze has taken over her brain: a fog as thick as the mist that on particularly cold days shrouds Matter Island: a fog she thought had evaporated for good by her leaving her motherland.

Inside her, glimmers of hope alternate with waves of deep sorrow. Emotions come and go, tears as well.

What if something was to happen to Maggie on the trip? Then it would be Maria's fault. Besides, if she doesn't go, Maggie will surely ditch her: she's can cave in or it's all over!

Luckily, the room stays empty like the rest of the school. Everybody has left for Easter.

On the bench, uninterrupted, Maria slowly manages to sort her train of thoughts into meaningful, coherent sentences. She remembers what she said; what she had carefully planned to say to best explain her decision.

How she apologized over and over and then used her age, mom, Helen, and as a last resort, Jay, as back up: as her backbone. How her mother finds Maria too young for such an adventure and so does Helen. And how the Taylors are looking forward to spending quality time with her at The Meadow Muse, especially Jay. He and a couple of his music-nerdy friends are in the early stages of forming a band; that indie band he's been rambling about for years. Jay would really like to run some ideas past her.

Although, Maria didn't mention how much she's looking forward to this, too: it's been forever since she and Jay had such a stretch of time together; happily high on life like they used to. Instead, she said that Maggie was welcome to come along again.

Despite Maria's effort, it did **not** go down well. In a split second, the expression on her dear friend's dolled-up face changed from passionate excitement to the despair and disillusionment of a toddler whose security blanket unexpectedly gets snatched away.

Emotions ran high. A virtual storm was unleashed on Maria who just stood there, mute and paralyzed. Each of Maria's good reasons, Maggie shot down with a counter point of view and an answer to why it wasn't. She didn't get it. First of all, Maggie didn't get why Maria had even told her mother; what a totally unnecessary roadblock. "We're not little kids anymore, baby M!" she reminded Maria, using a nickname, Gregg came up with recently which was funny only the first couple of times. Vaguely.

At long last, Maggie's attacks made a river of righteous rage arise from deep inside Maria:

"Don't call me that! Am I perhaps not the one who finished our last, so-called co-creative, project all by myself with absolutely no help from you? No, no, you were way too busy fooling around with your celebrity boyfriend, catering to his every need. What happened to the voice of Magdalena? What happened to those great ideas you used to have; it's like you don't think for yourself any-more. Why do you let your own dreams come second to Gregg's? It's not like he's doing the same for you!"

For a moment, Maggie stared stunned at her lamblike girlfriend suddenly showing teeth. She sought after a come-back, "Er, you've **got** to mingle with the right people to get anywhere - duh! Any-body with half a brain knows that! This is the city, you know; not some talent show at the village funfair. My Gregg's got bigger dreams than your dewy-eyed Jay with his precious boychoir, arty-farty school band or whatever. Gregg's dream is actually what I dream of, too. Should've known a baby like yourself who's never even had a real boyfriend wouldn't understand. I thought you as my best friend were in my corner on this. Well, silly me to think I could count on you!" Mag pouted with her head tilted, her eyes projectiles.

Mocking Maria's – the baby's – background, age and observa-tions is one thing: an occurrence she's grown used to. But then Maggie said those last words about Jay and topped it off with ques-tioning her loyalty. Casting doubt upon Maria's character hit a sore spot: a spot poked and prodded at before, on and off since she was a little girl. No wonder, it aches.

How on earth did it come to this?

In a haze, Maria gets up from the bench to wash her flushed, tear-stained face by the sink. The cold water soothes. The mirror, however, reflects a sad sight, and her eyes stray to avoid it. As the only one, a rebel soul has scribbled a phrase beside the mirror on a surprisingly squeaky clean wall for an Art School full of free-spir-ited creatives. Then; with multiple means of expression around here, why stoop to a bathroom wall?

The creative adult is the child who survived

Maria stares at the writings for a minute, the letters are pointy arrows shooting off the wall. This agony she's feeling, she's felt before. She knows her and Mag's dance: their dynamic, like the back of her hand. Maybe this pain doesn't mean anything other than if someone keeps poking at soft and delicate, defenseless, skin, it eventually causes bruises? Maybe the one constantly poking is the one to question?

It dawns on Maria that those words she just threw at Mag, with but a slight rewrite, might as well have been thrown at her own mother. Her eyes widen in the mirror.

When Maria finally steps out into the bright April sun, she's blinded by its sharpness. The schoolyard is deserted and so are chairs and wooden benches underneath apple trees on the verge of bloom, only an hour ago teeming with lunching, laughing pupils.

Maria sits down, gazing at the scenery. Soaking up the sun, she lets the rays warm her chilled, brittle being for a moment.

It's peaceful here, except for the ever-present birdsong of spring.

Abutting besties

Is she in today?

Maria hesitates in the doorway, peeking across the classroom. It doesn't look like it. As she drops down on her chair, temporary relief and anxious guilt battle within her. None of the sentiments get the upper hand, though: they just keep interchanging.

Maria never thought, she'd dread going to school at Fairview, yet here she is again.

She ought to be happy, it's a lovely day in May with summer break only weeks away. Her whole class is meeting up with a few teachers for a chat on the progress of their spring term projects, due next Monday. Well, the entire class except for Maggie...

Across the table from her, Christine cracks up about something Vivian: their always breezy Art Appreciation teacher, said. Maria didn't hear any of their banter. She gazes into Christine's warm smiling eyes, normally her classmate's beaming brown face is enough to cheer her up but not today.

"Why the long face?" Christine wants to know, "is something wrong?" her smooth forehead's wrinkled into a, way beyond her years, expression of motherly concern. Maria shakes her head with a grimacing smile. It's still too tender for her to talk about.

After the Easter episode, Maggie and Maria stopped interacting. They'll merely act civil whenever an encounter is unavoidable. In the beginning, Maria's begging eyes would search for her friend's to try and re-establish the connection, but Maggie's eyes, as well as her shoulder, are unmistakably turned and cold. Each time, Maria's had to fight back tears to first let them flow freely in the privacy of the restroom.

As everybody in class has been deeply involved in their different term projects this last month; projects which most of them
have chosen to work on from home, nobody has yet discovered
that the unbreakable Dotty Duo is no longer...

Until yesterday, Maria was, besides, unaware of what happened
at Easter.

When Maria got home that wretched Wednesday, she didn't
feel like letting Helen in on the mess, but a little later Jay came
home. He swung by her room, bright-eyed and in a brilliant mood,
soon noticing her less so state of being.

They had a good, long talk; the sort of raw and honest talk they
hadn't had in a while. Jay was able to put his feelings into words: "I
can't help but notice how Maggie basks in the attention, interest
and empathy you shower her with without fully reciprocating or
appreciating it. I'm sorry, but to me it seems, she simply takes it all
for granted..." Maria shed more tears. Sadly, his words rang true.

Jay supported her decision not to go, revealing a few disconcerting facts he'd heard about the band, especially Gregg, from
one of his music buddies. Things, he, at first, didn't want to tell
her because he didn't feel it was his place to do so or to diss a fellow musician. It would've been different if it was Maria, Gregg had
baited with an opportunity to join Vanguard Villains.

"Noblemen have a code of honor, you know," Jay glanced at his
nails, only half-joking: "we never rat out on one another."

"Class act, maybe... but, uh, does Gregg really deserve to be
put in such an honorable category simply for being a guy...?" she
looked him squarely in the eyes. Since Maria so fervently insisted,

Jay reluctantly gave in. Pacing the floor, he told her everything he knew while fidgety tucking and untucking his shirt into his pants.

Jay's friend Dave has a sister who's part of a clique of aspiring singers; those young girls are well-acquainted with Gregg's wily ways. According to her, his reputation is turning tarnished. To summarize, he's been around the block, riding on the band's success, promising this, that and the other. Maggie isn't exactly the first teenage girl hoping for more than a brief backing position. By now, they know his talk is empty.

Rumors linking the band to wild parties are persistent, too.

Jay suggested calling Maggie as soon as the initial upheaval had settled; no need to be pussyfooting around the issue. That same evening Maria did so, only to be rejected. Maggie didn't pick up the phone, but at long last Maria got hold of Rick. "Well, she says she doesn't want to speak to you," Rick sighed, "look, I'm going to put my foot down, here. If you don't want to go, fair enough, but then my little sis can't go, either. It's as simple as that."

This year, the Easter stay at the cottage wasn't up to standard of previous year.

The power of bass strings

Like a ghost, Maria's soul sister vanishes into the shadows.

A wall of silence arises between the former besties. Where once was ardent affection, setting ablaze bright flashes of inspiration and playful creativity, only a gap in the substantial size and shape

of that fire remains: a void, Maria know all too well and so habitually settles back into.

The guilt-ruts in her brain won't let her off the hook, though:
she keeps feeling bad. Why didn't she warn Maggie against Gregg?
How could she have prevented this?

Only after news about what went down at Easter finally reaches
Maria's ears, does she start accepting the situation, painful as it
is. Once more, the loose lips of Dave's sister spill, and she heard
about the incident through Lori. The aspiring and the old choir
singer are close by now. Maria has obviously been replaced, and no
wonder: the commonality of interest is undeniable. How can she
compete with a choir singing, street smart, super hip twenty-one-
year-old mom?

Apparently, the younger choir girl is so committed that she
crawled out the window of her brother's spare room early Maundy
Thursday, climbed down the gutter and ran off to join the touring
band.

The rebellious teenager didn't get far.

Rick, by a stroke of good luck; or the polar opposite in the eyes
of his little sis, woke up earlier than usual on a holiday. As soon
as he found Maggie's bed empty and her backpack missing, he
promptly phoned his father, who lives only a few blocks away.

Where the runaway was heading was no big mystery.

Maggie barely set foot on airport grounds before she was met
by her big brother and old man, waiting for her at the parking lot
by the shuttle bus stop. Her attachment to the musician was dis-

rupted but not for long. It was bound to happen: the inevitable coupling only got delayed.

According to several witnesses, Gregg and Mag have been seen canoodling in front of the city's high-end nightclub. And she always looks totally wasted, they say. It does happen, though, that the girl seen kissing the bass player isn't Maggie...

It's strange only to hear about your best friend through others, after having been her go-to listening ear for nearly two years. Who even ditched who? Probably the two of them grew apart, as adults call it, yet Maria feels she's failed Mag, failed her and was fast replaced.

Who knows, maybe Lori can save her?

~ Nine ~

The drop-out

Maria should've known their bond would break.

That's how it always goes. Happiness is a fleeting, ungraspable notion. It slips away.

Channeling all of her attention into finishing the term project is tested but falls flat. Busying herself doesn't work: she cannot concentrate and inspiration eludes her. Sheet after sheet of crumpled paper gets tossed in the bin. Frustrated, she leaves her desk to go outside. Why must everything turn to dust in her hands?

The night to Monday, she lies awake, staring into the darkness.

Jay has tried to help, and Helen and Christian have been extra attentive and kind, even while wrapping up their own work before the holidays. The rooting from the Taylors is greatly appreciated. If only their emotional investment in Maria yielded better results... Receiving so much support, surely **she** must be the missing link if nothing comes to fruition?

All that is growing within her is a deep longing for the simplicity of nature.

For nearly a week, sleep has been a luxury, she's had to learn to do without. Only the shortness of summer nights has made this situation bearable. As soon as the sun rises, Maria can be seen wandering the Taylors' misty garden; even before their rooster's proud morning crowing. Being up and about early doesn't automatically lead to any desired outcome, though. Come Sunday evening, she's still got nothing to show for it.

And nothing is what she delivers on Monday.

For once, Margaret looks concerned when Maria, in a surprisingly steady voice, tells her the news. The wiped-out student deliberately approached her last, after all of her classmates. "Um, I actually heard from Maggie yesterday..." their teacher, wearing a becoming denim dress taking years off her age, hesitates, rubbing her eyes, "she said not to tell anyone yet, but if you don't already know, I think you, of all people, deserve to hear it..."

She sweeps her chestnut bangs behind the ears, "You know, I won't be able to grade any of you now, and that this is, unfortunately, going to lower your final grades. However, you can still rectify the situation, if you put all of your heart and soul into the critical final term project next year."

Margaret breathes in, searching for the right words: "Descending to a lower level to keep a troubled friend company has nothing to do with true friendship, Maria: you do know that, right?" Maria's ears perk up," Uh, not sure, I know what you mean?" the fog in her mind begins to clear.

"Please tell me what Mag said!" she can't contain her curiosity any longer.

"Well, Maggie, like you, said she was very sorry, but that she was unable to submit the assigned term project. To be honest, she sounded somewhat inebriated..." Margaret walks over to open up a window with less bounce in her steps than normal. "In fact, Maggie won't be coming back," she sighs profusely, leaning against one of the desks. Her eyes turn sad as they inspect the glum face of the other girl, letting herself down.

"Maggie's a remarkable girl who unfortunately has a lot going on at the home front. Probably, she should have joined our music wing. It seems blatantly obvious, and if her father hadn't insisted otherwise, she would have. I just figured, she would end up transitioning; not jump ship entirely... She's been able to charm her way through the last couple of years, never admitting to how she was really doing. It's only recently her attendance dropped dangerously and the true state of affairs became clear."

Deep in thoughts, Margaret stares out the window, "Look, I don't know what's been going on between the two of you. At first, you were clearly so in tune with each other: two peas in a pod, so playful and creative. But I guess lately you've both been putting on a front?"

The lump in her throat makes it hard for Maria to answer. She sits down at the desk, biting the nail on her thumb whilst getting chills; frost is threatening to overtake her again. Shuddering, she wraps both arms around her t-shirt clad torso.

"I never understood what she saw in Gregg. She wouldn't listen to me, though. And me; I'm so insecure and didn't know how to help her," she whispers, frowning at the table. "I honestly believed we were alike, too, but as it turns out, Maggie's way of coping is different from mine. I couldn't follow her there. Can't you do something, Margaret? Please!" hopeful, Maria lifts her gaze.

"I really wish, I could, Maria," Margaret strokes her pupil's shivering shoulder, "but as Maggie has now officially dropped out of Fairview, there isn't much more I can do, besides talk to her parents and suggest they get some professional help. I will call her mother later today. Wish, I had known a little sooner how bad things were..."

"I knew, I should have told you," Maria bursts into tears, "it's all my fault..." her voice goes faint. Margaret softly squeezes the dis-traught young girl's upper arm," Chin up, dear, of course, it's not your fault! We cannot fix or rescue others. Not really. We can't save them from feeling painful emotions; from doing their own inner healing work. We can only be patient and compassionate when, or if, they choose to do so. Issues like addiction run deeper, often originating in the family. There are reasons as to why we are at-tracted to the people we are, reasons our logical mind seldom un-derstands..." she lovingly hands her pupil a paper hanky, holding space for her tears to subside.

"Some cope in ways more destructive than others... So, how do **you** cope, then?" her teacher's eyes are sincere and insistent.

Maria's thrown off for a moment. Margaret goes on, "I mean, you often act so self-sufficient, hardly ever seem to require any-body's help. Even I thought you were doing fine after those lovely chats we had in your freshman year," the tenderness melts away Maria's defenses. Once again, her teacher's superb maternal in-stinct has kicked in.

Her pupil resists receiving nurturance, though, "I guess, I'm just too darned used to pasting a smile on my face, however bad I actually feel!" Margaret's smile drops, and Maria regrets her outburst. No one deserves it less. "Sorry, don't mean to yell at you..." she's close to tears again. "That's okay. Anger is a valid human reaction. Potentially useful. It's a cut above guilt, fear and shame, for sure. Don't think I don't understand your frustration," Margaret remains calm and compassionate: "To always wear an agreeable "good-girl" mask comes with a price, dear; like any prolonged pretense. In the end, it can make you sick. Even if the outer world and society tends to reinforce this kind of sickness, by all means, try to stop yourself from slipping it on too often," she suggests serious-faced.

"So, you're still hiding your true feelings?"

Maria sighs, "It sorta just happens, you know, after years of practice: it's second nature. Particularly if I'm already in a slump. At times, speaking about things takes way more energy: it can mess with my emotional balance for, literally, days!" she peeks shyly at her teacher, grimacing, "It's like, I need crazy amounts of time to process my emotions and sort things through..."

Margaret nods, "Of course. I often like to name the most sensitive people in society "front feelers": the courageous ones processing the emotional debris of humanity after centuries of emotional suppression, denial or trauma. One day, I even believe we'll be recognized for our important role as such. But no martyrdom; we don't have to feel things through alone, you know, nor do we need to keep things to ourselves, even long after sorting them through. Please practice reaching out and sharing once in a while," she smiles affectionately. Unprotesting, Maria rubs her forehead, reciprocating the smile. In spite of recent events, her mouth hasn't

forgotten how, "Thinking about it, I guess my main means of escape are music or books, and if I'm honest: food. But even if he's
often busy, I do have my good friend, Jay, to talk to. Oh, and his
mom, too!"

"Glad to hear it, Maria. Yes, Helen is a sensible person to turn
to. As for Maggie: she **is** very vulnerable right now, but she'll get
through this and back on her feet: a young person with a talent
like hers, brimming with lust for life! I feel confident she's going
to find her way," Margaret starts packing her pupils' term papers
into a big brown leather bag.

Midway, she stops and looks up, "Um, this is just a hunch, but I
suggest looking up the term "co-dependency" and then let's have
more lovely chats next year, okay? And by the way; don't ever
think you're not equally remarkable, Maria. That light you see in
Maggie, lives in you, too, or you wouldn't be able to recognize it.
To tend our own light; at times only the tiniest of flames, shielding
and cupping our hands around it, is our main task in life. Beyond
all else, beyond all the other, trivial stuff we have to do."

Margaret's tone is as soft as a fuzzy blanket swaddling a newborn. The sleep-deprived teenager blushes and closes her eyes.
Sadly, she feels too tired and miserable to fully take in the wisdom
and praise her teacher offers.

"Maybe you could also call Lori," she quickly diverts the topic.
"Lori?" Margaret's eyebrows rise.

"No, wait! I'll do that," Maria's suddenly certain of what to do.

"All right, then!" Margaret smiles, lifting the heavy leather bag
off the ground, ready to head home. Then she hesitates, "I'll un-

derstand it if you don't feel like meeting up with the others on Friday when they receive their evaluations; that's okay by me."

Maria nods with a grateful smile. Together, they slowly walk toward the door.

"Try to enjoy summer, darling. Next year, you'll sail through your exams, no doubt!" Margaret laughs reassuringly, "come on, let's go home. And sleep tight now, you," she winks. "Thanks a lot. Gee, I certainly hope so... Have a lovely summer, Margaret!" Maria waves goodbye as they part ways outside the classroom.

She stays for a minute, watching her teacher walk down the light-filled hallway, watching the cherished female figure get smaller until her middle-aged mentor and friend pushes through the solid mahogany double doors and disappears from sight.

The sound of them slamming behind her echoes through the empty hall.

Adrift on a baby blue sea

What a bummer this summer's become. Still, she tries to stick to Margaret's advice.

If it wasn't for The Meadow Muse and Jay, no doubt Maria would be even bluer. The comforting company, diving into various creative pursuits and recharging in nature, prevent her from drowning in a sea of sadness.

Jay and Maria walk along the shoreline almost every morning, talking and skipping stones. While he's still not that fond of the water, she'll sometimes have a quick swim. In the cottage garden, she helps Ray pick the early veggie harvest. Enjoying having an audience, even if only one, he passionately talks about permaculture gardening: "Mere mother wit for folks, flora & fauna!" he takes a bite of a radish, dirt and all.

Maria asks about the cottage which she knows is now more than fifty years old. It still looks so beautiful and modern with its rooftop windows: was it difficult to design or construct? Ray nods," This place was the first real test of my architectural skills. It was challenging to get all the details right, for sure, but so worth it: a home built to last!" he pulls off the beret to scratch his hair, "heh, how we men love building monuments, while what good mothers provide often go unnoticed... Patiently nurturing a fragile seed to fruition needs a feminine approach, or saying it differently: attentive tender care is a crucial component when it comes to making any living being thrive."

Playful, Ray puts his beret on Maria's head. It instantly drops down, covering her eyes and nose. "Ew, your hat is a bit smelly, Ray, don't you ever wash it?" They both laugh.

Seeking solitude, the teen girl explores the wilderness around the cottage on her own. Most afternoons, she escapes in a book, lounging on a blanket in the middle of a lush nearby meadow, she's found. Maria's been neglecting her love of reading. Sneakily, the draining drama of her actual life replaced the pleasurable dramas of fictitious stories. She has to somehow switch it back around again.

The sweet scent of chamomile and sensing the warm sunshine on her shoulders gifts her a blessed calm, as nature's medicine always does. Flashbacks from the time Mag was here, emerge now and then, though. She can't help it. Gosh, the fun they had...

Visiting Matter Island this summer is out of the question. Right now, she's in no shape to deal with those familiar faces; cannot stomach enduring her nosy mother's cross-examinations or her father's mood swings and prickliness, pestering the house. The missed term project turns out a convenient excuse. Her parents reckon Maria must've been lackadaisical and thus reluctantly accept it when their daughter claims she better study to make up for this and not fall behind in class.

The commotion with Maggie won't pass Maria's lips. Her throat constricts if she as much as attempts to mention her name when she's on the phone with her mother.

Talking to Lori also turns out more difficult than expected. The fresh young mom reacts somewhat standoffish when Maria introduces herself on the phone. "Yeah, I've heard a bit about you, a little bit..." Lori sounds self-assured and slightly on guard: what she's heard can't be only good. Maria swallows, feeling like an over-emotional, awkward twelve-year-old playing pretend. "How is Maggie, do you know? Uhm, I hope everything is all right?" her voice breaks, ruining the thin veneer of breeziness. She lets go of all pretense.

"I worry if everything is okay with her? If Gregg is treating her well and her dad also. Because... because: maybe if they don't and her emotions get the better of her, she'll maybe com...compensate and numb out by drinking too much?" Maria's tongue trips over the therapeutic term.

"That's kind of an indelicate thing to say. I don't think Maggie is drinking more than most teenagers her age; you better not be gallivanting around, broadcasting all over that she's an alcoholic!" Lori's voice is harsh and hits her like a blow in the belly.

"No, no, that's not what I meant!" the unexpected outlash makes her panic, "You're twisting my words, I would never say or do anything so mean!" Maria gets dizzy.

"Well, you better not..." Lori's mildly appeased, "I don't know who is twisting what, but Maggie is fine; didn't fit in at your posh high school, anyway. She's already a part of the music business. If you must know, she'll likely be credited alongside yours truly on the next Vanguard Villains album. Ahem, I'll make sure to send her your best, all right? Bye, bye now."

The line goes dead. Maria stares at the phone.

What is the truth?

~ Ten ~

A fall from favor

"Jeanette Patrickson"

The chalk signature on the blackboard blurs before Maria's eyes.

"I'm sure we'll get along smashingly!" the foreign beauty smiles wide with glossy lips. Her hairstyle is beautiful, too: braided all the way from the top of her scalp down to the middle of her back. Running shoes on her feet and training pants. A sporty outfit. She's blond, tanned and doesn't look a day beyond twenty-five. Eric and all the other guys in here; even Clive who leaped undauntedly out of the closet in their sophomore year, seem more awake than she remembers any of them ever having been. Jeanette has grabbed everyone's attention.

While Christine also looks dejected when the two of them exchange a nonplussed glance, Maria's apparently the only one in class who feels like she was just hit over the head with a hammer. Granted, a nordic-goddess-looking one but the knock still hits awfully hard.

Gah, and she who was so eager to see Margaret again!

After initial resistance since neither of her parents is an addict, Maria read up on co-dependency which turned out to ignite so many lightbulbs it nearly blew her fuse. Among other eye-opening facts, she learned that using prescribed sedatives as means of numbing can have tricky side effects, too. She, besides, discovered who it was she originally felt so compelled, even obliged, to support and save...

In the course of summer, Maria's also pondered what could possibly be so remarkable about herself, apart from maybe the color and unruliness of her hair? In short, she's bursting with burning questions she was hoping to ask Margaret.

This sucks big time.

Maria hears only half of what the gorgeous new creative writing teacher says. But it seems, Margaret's husband was offered a sudden promotion: a raise too substantial to refuse, entailing transfer abroad. Ergo they had to make the on-the-spot decision to relocate asap. "They hired me last week!" Jeanette laughs again. She does that a lot; speaks fast, too. Maria has a hard time keeping track of what their new teacher says.

In the cafeteria at lunchtime, Maria's head is in a haze.

Christine agrees that it sucks but says she quite likes Jeanette's optimistic attitude and the youthful dynamism the newest addition to the teaching staff is bringing along: it's a breath of fresh air. "And wow, isn't she like, super stunning! She could easily be a model, I think. In fact, I bet she already is!" Maria's normally laid-back and levelheaded classmate is excited, her eyes sparkle as she hurls a spoonful of peas on her salad.

Maria's not sure whose betrayal is the worst: Margaret's for disappearing without saying goodbye or her classmates for redirecting all the well-deserved admiration and affection they felt for a beloved teacher to somebody new in the snap of a finger.

How fickle human hearts can be.

Helen didn't know anything about Margaret leaving, she swears when Maria comes home. She's as surprised and sad as her bonus daughter, "It must've been a necessary fast decision, or she would never have done it. As far as I know, Margaret was super content and well-liked by everyone at Fairview. Can't believe she's giving all that up," Helen shakes her head in disbelief and sighs, "she'll be sending you one of her special letters soon, you'll see: one that explains everything." Despite her modern mindset, Margaret's famous for her longstanding love of crafting personal, poetic handwritten letters. Quite quaint.

When it comes down to it, maybe Margaret isn't so different from mom, after all, Maria figures, begrudgingly. The bitter thought gets lodged in her head.

Come rain or shine, life goes on as it always does. It also becomes apparent, that the view on weather conditions entirely is a matter of whose perspective is made to count.

At school, a subtle discrepancy slowly grows between Maria and the ever-smiling Jeanette Patrickson. And along with it, a veering away from her classmates happens since everybody else is infatuated with their pretty young teacher.

The new mainstay in class clearly has a brilliant mind and as early as in high school became editor of a trendsetting monthly magazine. Before the age of twenty, she won a prestigious literary prize for young novelists, and she's also, despite her youth, had several short stories published. Jeanette's father is a highly reputed literary professor teaching at the city's grand old university while her mother is art director at a leading advertising agency, besides being his publicist. A pedigree that can't be denied.

Already, Maria has a hard time understanding the parlance and pathways of relating in academia: the long-established frameworks. It's so unfamiliar and so... intellectual?

Helen is right, though. In September, Maria receives a lovely, light-scented letter in the mail, handwritten and even on handmade paper. The envelope is stamped in some faraway country she hardly knows.

"I'm ever so sorry for having to leave you all, particularly you, Maria, in this manner. In troubling times, make sure to lean on Helen, dear. Don't lose heart: remember I have faith in you even when it eludes you. Trust yourself, never forget how worthy and wise you are." Margaret's words are sweet and heartening, and she's even written her phone number at the bottom as a lifeline.

There's already a distance, though. Maria's eyes moist, but the frozen feeling around her chest, preventing the pumping organ inside from wasting vital life force on yet another lost connection, is already set in place. One simply has to withdraw to lick one's wounds and come to grips with the loss. At least, she has to do so.

At school, Maria passes on the overall message but doesn't show anyone the letter.

What makes school bearable, now and then even enjoyable, is mainly Christine and Maria's continual friendly chatter and quirky inside jokes. Despite their differences, the two of them have always been in sync. Christine is a busy young woman, though. Besides school, she's got friends, family and an auspicious student job at a publishing house downtown. The job was arranged by her mother: a debuting author, doing okay. Twenty-four hours a day is scarcely enough.

As the year progresses, the gap widens between herself and most of her classmates who all orbit around Jeanette like was she the sun, itself. Maria, on the contrary, can't help but notice a lack of accord between the two of them.

Jeanette enjoys lively class debates with lots of mental acrobatics and so encourages her pupils to conjure up as many counter viewpoints to those of their classmates as possible; the more, the better. The classroom transforms into an imaginary courtroom where Eric and a couple of other boys are court jesters. Plenty of laughs, although quite a few cheap. Sarcasm. Wordplay turning to swordplay: all wit and no heart. And no mention of wooing the muse of course; likely their young teacher doesn't believe in any such unpredictable creatures...

Anyhow, as apparently the only one in class missing something, Maria, no doubt, must be mistaken. Helen rather likes her new colleague, too, "I'm sure Jeanette means well. She's probably just trying a little bit too hard... she **is** very young, you know."

The young woman's all about progressiveness. Thinking outside the box is an integral part of being creative, she teaches. Creative work should be thought-provoking: preferably breaking new ground. To grab people's attention from the get-go is rule number one, she says, whether one writes fiction or commercials. It's a known fact that a fair share of the school's lit nerds often goes on to work as copywriters at advertising agencies. State-of-the-art literature should explore and express cutting edge matters, Jeanette enthuses in a monologue about how pioneering writers will form the future landscape of literature. "Fostering new pioneers like you is the main purpose of Fairview!" a fire burns inside the ambitious teacher's eyes.

The students' faces mirror their new mentor's. They feel proud to be enrolled here, eager to prove themselves worthy of such honor.

While Jeanette's size-zero exterior looks the epitome of delicate femininity, her inner workings soon seep through, revealing a differing disposition. She gives off the air of an archetypical Viking more than of the Elven princess she resembles. Every person's energy is like a language with its very own signature, beneath their spoken one. Maria senses these transmissions. Despite how undeniably engaged their teacher is in her pupils, the intuitive teen, to find her own stance, needs space and time to go inside. This process typically gets steam-rolled, and Maria, inevitably, second-guesses herself.

To her perhaps most sensitive and perceptive student, Jeanette's agile energy feels off, bordering pushy. Her whole approach rubs Maria the wrong way, making her anxious. Weirdly, it's as if Jeanette might be driven by a devil of the same pesky sort as the one driving Maria's father. Switching job title from fish factory foreman to carpenter only ever altered things on the surface...

One wintery day in late November, Jeanette calls Maria out on being too sentimental and touchy-feely in her essays. In a light-hearted tone, of course, using other phrases: "Present-day writers experiment with lots of cool writing styles. Brainstorm more, and let your writing express and explore wider topics like, for example, our society or current issues in the world. The private sphere of relationships and emotions is sadly overused, even if it easily produces corny fiction or a trashy novel: often by the hands of our gender, I'm sorry to say," her face is fresh, the words matter-of-factly.

The sense of creative playfulness at school disappears, at least for Maria.

From now on, the sixteen-year-old reverts to an overwrought copycat making futile attempts at changing to fit the setting. This bygone behavior Maria readily shed when leaving the island, never thinking she would have to take it up again. To not feel cast outside the circle of belonging, she adapts as best she can, though.

With both Mag and Margaret gone, Maria slowly slips out on the fringe. She retracts to being mostly an observer again. They were like a passport to Fairview, helping her feel as much of a worthwhile participant here as the others: their equal. Now, she'll catch herself comparing, separating herself. She shrinks, going ever quieter. Maria's not the only introvert in class, but no one else seems to need quite as much time to ponder things or come up with the right words.

Maria watches Karen and Rae chat with Jeanette. Both of these fine young women come from the upper-middle class. Well-read and from well-educated families; parents who went to college. To them, effortless interacting, throwing about articulate, high brow expressions, is just a matter of course.

They fit in seamlessly. **They** belong; deserve to be here.

Maria's struggle at measuring up in class, in its own sour way, at least serves as a distraction from ruminating about Maggie.

Then, in the middle of December in passing a newsstand, a tabloid headline on the sidewalk stares her in the face: "THE VILLAINS WREAKING HAVOC!" On the cover: a photo of Gregg looking hammered, groping a famous model. Classy.

Maria has no choice but to buy that sleazy paper, soon holding a copy in her winter-numb hands. She reads stories of lavish parties getting out of hand; reckless behavior. One of the guys, no mention of who, apparently trashed their hotel room after a gig, and the police got involved. Looks like they're busy living up to the rock star myth...

The one credited for the caustic article is no other than her former friend's father. In seeing it, Maria's throat constricts. Where's Maggie in all of this?

Not long after, following a Christmas party at her job, Christine catches a glimpse of their old classmate at a fancy club. She reports that Mag looked pretty wasted, but that there was no Gregg in sight. Lori and two unknown, older-looking broads were with her. Christine didn't feel like approaching them.

Both sightings stir things up again.

That Christmas on Matter Island, Maria, in not too many details, manages to explain the situation to her mother. Her father knows nothing of Maggie: no need to bring her up to him. To keep pretending, under her mother's probing eyes, that her former bestie is still around, is not possible. Tears are unavoidable. Mom comforts her upset daughter, shocked to hear that Mag dropped out. "Oh, my, even she who sounded so gifted? Sad to say it, but that girl has now lost **my** respect! I guess, the luring dangers of a big city sometimes ruin the weaker ones. You're better off without her, Kitty cat!" Like in the movies, mom believes all is now lost for the strayed heroine.

Her daughter is too spent to object.

How Maria misses Margaret's calming presence, her maturity and depth. Not to mention, her passion for words as poetic conveyers of emotion rather than worldly ideas and concepts. If Margaret was an exquisite aged red wine, rich with subtle layers, their new teacher is more of the cooler, cheaper sparkling one: fine and fast to provide a buzz on a summer day but undeniably unsatisfactory for a winter's night.

Anywho, comparing past favor with present-day reality is pointless.

It doesn't take long, though, before Jeanette's conceptual writing prompts ignite little to no sparks in Maria. The words they yield sound contrived, almost phony. She feels her confidence shrink for each time an essay comes back with her teacher's scribblings all over, full of exclamation signs; even if softened by a smiley.

By the end of the school year, the nail on Maria's pinky could hold what's left.

An order too tall

Maria waits with bated breath, opening and closing her sweaty palms in her lap.

Time has come for being handed their crucial final year project, and the energy in class is tense. It's a lovely day of spring, still, Maria feels cold: benumbed. She has chosen to work on her own again which many of her classmates have, too, among them, also Christine.

Independence and collaboration are regarded equal here at Fairview: a mere matter of personal preference or style. One of the things, Maria's always loved about her school.

When the assignment lands on her desk, however, and she reads the project heading, it becomes blatantly clear that it's got Jeanette's fingerprint all over:

"1 PLAY: 5 FULLY-FORMED ADAPTATIONS"
"Write a short but original theatrical piece that pays homage to your home country's constitution (8-10 pages). Then rewrite your play in additional 4 different creative styles while also exploring alternative constitutions: genres are of your own choosing. The distinction between each adaptation must be crystal clear and each one must involve detailed suggestions for staging, costumes, musical backing, etc, etc."

Maria quietly gasps and her heart sinks. This is no surprise yet still she can't breathe.

Even with six weeks to accomplish the task, she knows she'll be writhing like an out-of-water fish in death throes. Brainstorming for hours on end or not!

Maria looks around at her classmates. Christine stares concentrated at the paper with a frowning face, trying to grasp the extent of this task. Most of the other girls, Karen and Rae included, sigh, looking at each other with ambivalent faces. Eric whistles: "That's quite an assignment you've handed us, here, Miss Patrickson..." his eyebrows rise over sharp green eyes as he runs his fingers through his brand new short hairdo. Beside him, Clive throws his hands dramatically up in the air in capitulation.

If those guys are intimidated, then **she** is definitely doomed!

"Come on, you guys!" Jeanette won't hear of any fuss; "sure, it's challenging, and so it should be: you're ready for this! The examiner and I can't wait to read all of your sensational scripts in their fivefold versions. Get ambitious and get to work!"

The pupils split into small murmuring groups or stay solo. Some leave. Christine and Maria exchange a few animated words, tell each other to "break a leg" and part ways. "I'll be calling you repeatedly!" Christine laughs as she unlocks the chain on her bike.

Maria knows Christine most likely won't be. With her foot wedged in the door to the publishing world, supported by an author mother who has all the right connections; Maria's favorite friendly face in class is likely going to do just fine.

And even if he wishes to, Jay can't help much out, either. He's in the throes of final term project, too: composing a musical piece with Dave and a cellist named Dennis.

Somehow, she has to figure this one out on her own.

On the way home, Maria swings by the bakery on the corner of Main Street. They make the most divine carrot cake with cream cheese frosting, there. She usually only does this on days when Helen isn't home until later. Her city mama loves a yummy cake, too, but she would worry if she saw Maria eat half of a whole one. Naturally.

It seems most city folks are conscious of eating healthily. At first, it was a bit foreign to Maria. Back on the island, they've always just eaten whatever the grocery next door offered, preferably at a discount. Eating well is eating heavy foods such as grandma's tasty but rich, old-fashioned cuisine: meat, sugar, flour, cream and fat. Preferably heaps of it. The potato: pretty much the only veggie not in the doghouse.

After Maria moved here, all the rich, processed foods that soothe and ground you or provide plenty of calories for hard work, besides the sweets boosting your mood with a quick sugar rush, started to no longer agree with her. Not while she's here, anyway.

City folks like their food lesser, lighter and greener; the Taylors, too. The change in diet influenced Maria greatly until she got used to being a little more lightheaded and lighter on her feet. A few months in, and she loved the "light as a feather" feeling it gave her. After each island visit, she can't wait to shed that dense pile of saturated fat, starch and sugar from her system, even if while there, eating it also seems to help in putting her a par with her family and the rest of the islanders.

It serves as a nice and necessary buffer.

Floating about as light as a feather just won't cut it on her ancestral island. A gust of the violent west wind so often sweeping the isle will soon blow you completely apart. Sensitive residents often need a bit of padding fat cushioning them against their less so environment. Funny, how the same stuff serving Maria in a disturbingly gratifying way on the island, somehow is too heavy or hard to digest once back in the city.

Here, it only makes her feel sluggish.

Many girls at school are vegetarians, only eat organic food or are, at least, very picky about what they feed their, more often than not, skinny young bodies. Since Jeanette's arrival, a couple of girls in class have besides lost weight, Maria has noticed.

Strangely, their new teacher has the exact opposite effect on her.

If need be, bakeries are still plenty in the city...

~ Eleven ~

A lesson learned

"I am so sorry for having to bring you this news."

Jeanette's voice on the phone is pitying: "It didn't feel right only sending your papers back to you; spelled out in black and white can look a bit harsh... Uhm, sadly, we are not able to let you pass, Maria. The examiner agreed with me. You did not deliver what was asked of you: the submitted script, even if engaging and over seventy pages long, doesn't sufficiently meet our requirements. Ahem, it isn't the end of the world, you know, Maria, please don't dwell on this bump in the road. No, we have to get up on our feet again and move on!" the phrase sounds trite coming from a twenty-five-year-old mouth. Jeanette shifts tone and speed of voice, eager to get to her point, "Maybe consider a different career path than this one? Now that you know more, you've got the chance to make an informed decision, eh? I hear you've got amazing drawing skills!" on the finishing note, Maria's teacher dials the perkiness up a notch.

In the meantime, Maria's mind has gone blank, "You're probably right... and thanks," niceties cover for her while holding back tears.

"Well, all right then!" Jeanette inhales, relieved to have done her duty. She wishes her, freshly flunked and still stunned, student all the best and hangs up.

Maria's thoughts start racing like mad. She put no less than all of her heart and soul into that play: a play about a rupture in the friendship between two teen girls. A sad, emotive story not un-like her and Mag's. She delved deep into the creative process and wrote and wrote and wrote. In the end, she felt a bit batty but also... cleansed?

In a desperate attempt at meeting the assigned requirements, Maria aptly titled it: "The Constitution of a Failed Friendship". Alas, she fears the script's only cemented her rep as a hopeless softie...

More than anything, what this final term project did for her was lead her down a winding road of unexpected self-discovery. A sense of rightness slowly emerged while she wrote, a certainty that soothed her guarded heart and calmed her hazy, busy brain.
Every disjointed thought or frazzled feeling settled down, her whole being went still.

Maria now knows that grasping at low-hanging fruits has never been her main reason for being creative. She needs to thoroughly explore her subject and trust her instincts.

What compels her is to carefully climb the symbolical inner tree, led by subtle cues and intuitive hunches, in the hopes of dis-covering a creative fruit with **her** signature on it. Even if the iden-tified "fruit" dangles dangerously from the farthest of branches.
To trust the deep well of her psyche and follow inner prompts to artistic completion: THIS is her thing!

The revelation left Maria awestruck, body buzzing. Truth tingles.

Writing the play felt really healing, but it seems her writing is awful. Just.... garbage? Despite what Margaret said, being true to herself didn't pay off.

This is so unfair!

Maria can't think straight. In her mind's eye, a flash of Fairview appears, flooded in sunlight. Then her school collapses in a blast of dust, leaving but a huge pile of bricks.

Luckily, no one's home. Numbed, she walks out into the garden. Air is of the essence. Air and peace. Nature. No other humans to relate to, only Spot trotting along beside her. He's becoming ever more sedate and slow-going; both his eyesight and hearing have decreased considerably over the last year. Maria lets herself drop down behind a big Butterfly Bush. Spot nestles up against her, resting his little graying face on her thigh. She starts to cry. The dog gazes confused at her with his brown puppy eyes, blurred by age.

Soon, Spot will be gone, too.

Lying in the grass, a storm of gasping sobs, a long time coming, overtakes the teenage girl from head to toe. Maria's, presently, tubby torso covered only by a cerise tank top shudders and goosebumps spread fast across bare skin exposed to the elements on her budding body. Freezing, she tugs the fabric of her canvas skirt tightly around her legs.

She blew it. Her one shot of making something of herself.

Slowly, flower fragrances along with the physical sensation of solid ground right beneath that grass Maria lies upon, graciously lend her some primordial strength. She sits up straight, wraps both arms around her knees and pushes them close to her chest. Her throat still hurts, but her eyes dry. Hopelessness shifts to emptiness. Quiet. Maybe, if she can keep herself together, she'll be able to keep a shred of power no matter what her future entails?

Right under her nose, a row of busy ants scurry by beneath blades of grass. She looks on as the last one in line ambitiously wrestles with a pebble ten times its own size but, weakened by the weight, soon falls behind its faster mates who carry lesser burdens. Why not just drop it and pick up a smaller, manageable piece? Bees and beautiful butterflies flutter around the bushes; only now, Maria notices. The insects move about to the crystalline tones of a twittering bird, nearby.

She used to delight in all things peculiar and pretty, however small; easily attuning to reverie and awe. What happened to that poetical lens? What's happened to her?

Maria's stomach hurts. It's not that time of the month yet: did she eat something bad, or is it hunger? She gets on her feet and walks inside the house again, on the hunt for food, recalling how Helen baked a chocolate cake the other day.

If she hurries, she can finish it off before her city mama comes back.

Another call, different message

"Hello... are you there?"

Overwhelmed by emotions, Maria can't get a word out. Finally, a faint, rusty sounding "Yes," rolls of her tongue. She peeks at the patio doors to the garden. Like yesterday, Helen, Jay, Christian and Lisa, who came back home from inter-railing last night and has a lot of juicy stories to tell, still sit outside after a hearty dinner, chatting drowsily under the blazing July sun. It won't be dark for hours.

To be safely out of sight, she lies down on the rattan lounge chair behind one of the bamboo blinds in the bay window. Her legs are a little shaky, too.

Awkward silence until Maria quietly asks Mag how she's been? Her long-lost friend starts telling how the last year unfolded for her. In a slow, broken voice, she confesses that she was so mad at Maria but also that she's really missed her, and how she sees things differently now. "How so?" Maria wants to know.

"Uh, it didn't work out with Gregg. Or we are still in touch because he is one of few who gets what I'm going through since his old man was known as the town drunk... But our fling ended kinda bad," Mag chews on each word before spitting it out, as if she has to have a taste to access if it's the proper one. She sounds unlike her former fiery self. The pity momentarily impairs Maria, who waits as Mag composes herself. "Annoyingly, you were right. Even if it was crazy fun for a while, in the end, it became more crazy than fun... I was putty in Gregg's hands and slowly lost my will and voice in all that celebrity nonsense. My therapist helped me realize it..."

The disclosure surprises Maria, "You're in therapy?"

"Yeah..." there's a deep sigh at the other end. "Margaret per-suaded me, even though I fought it for the longest time," Mag sounds resigned, "besides being on a strong regiment of pills, it seems I need to learn to deal with those blasted feelings without instantly reaching for a drink. No more drowning my sorrows. I am, sorry to say, not 100% there, yet. I've had some setbacks... it's rough."

"It's a good start," Maria's voice is mushy, "And it's not your fault. So many of us were never taught how to deal with hard emo-tions in a healthy way and will simply numb them any which way we know how; you're not alone. Uh, I wish to confess something, too. It wasn't only you, I was infatuated by that glitzy world, too. So blinded. At first, anyway. Now, I feel I should have done more, insisted more; warned you earlier on."

Maria takes no notice of the Taylors outside anymore; all of her attention goes to picking back up a disrupted conversation with a friend.

Mag is not the only one in therapy; her whole family is. "Dad accepted it only after spewing a bunch of curse words," she grins, sounding like her old self, "at first, he was having none of it but guess losing his job over crossing the line one too many times, helped in getting him on board... Urgh, it was sooo uncomfortable in the beginning. Eventually, we got to the core of things. It's like the ghost of grandma was still around and as it turned out and even worse: grandpa's grouchy old one!" Maggie doesn't hold any-thing back. In usual melodramatic fashion, she starts telling all about it.

The initial trust is restored, and the two of them have an awful lot of catching up to do. A setting sun peers through the blinds and turns to streaks of light orange, softly caressing Maria's face. She has to shift position often, after a while, the rattan starts pinching her skin.

"Uh, I'll be leaving the city Monday... going back to the island," the dismal fact sinks a little more in, becomes dreadfully real, as Maria says the words aloud. After four years, this place has, thanks to the Taylors, become close to home. Where does she belong?

"What! No, that can't be true - spill!" Mag gasps.

"Well, no one is kicking me out. Lisa's back from traveling, though, needing her old room back until she finds a job and a new flat. I don't want to exhaust the Taylors' goodwill: they've done so much, already. Mom is, besides, guilting me, saying how she looks forward to getting to know her own daughter again. Jay, Lisa and the rest of the family will be sending me off in style with a casual Farewell party at the cottage tomorrow. I'm sure you are welcome if you feel like coming?"

"Oh, thanks, but I feel a bit too unstable for any kind of party, to be honest. Guess, I don't fully trust myself. Hope that's okay?" Maria does understand. Mag exhales, "Wow, I can't believe you're leaving. It's nice Jay passed with flying colors but that you flunked: you with your love of the written word? So unfair! That Jeanette sure sounds annoying; better suited for a runway than a teaching position, if you ask me. A pain in the "you-know-what", however smart or foxy, still a butt-pain!" she snorts and Maria laughs. Her heart swells, the glimpse of her friend's spunky spirit is so great.

"Why don't you get a job in the city?" Mag's question follows naturally.

"Uh, I wouldn't know where to go," a familiar pang of fear for the future hits Maria. Her self-esteem yo-yos a lot, just like before she moved to the city, maybe even more. Back to square one. Feeling like a hopeless case, she aims the spotlight back on Mag, "I honestly don't know where I belong anymore.... What's your plan; surely, it involves singing professionally? Please don't forget about Magdalena."

"Well, the band's label never paid me a penny for all the time and energy I gave them. I learned certain valuable things about the music scene, sure, but mostly I had to fit in and deliver whatever they needed from me. A tough lesson for this rookie! Now I'm actually glad I never signed a contract. Right now, I need to pick myself up from that dark hole I fell down when Gregg cheated on me. Find my feet again, as well as my own voice. Take things at my own pace. I feel like starting afresh, maybe even come up with a brand new stage name..." Mag sounds hopeful albeit a bit bewildered.

"So you should. Please promise to never give up singing because that would be a tragedy!" Maria's outburst surprises herself. She means every word, though, "I never understood your eagerness to give away the best of you. So easily and even for free."

Mag chuckles; "I won't, promise. But as for throwing one's talents away, it seems I could ask you the same question?"

It's Maria's turn to part snort, part sigh: "Fair enough. Yes, I've got work to do in that area, too. You know, while we've been apart, I've come to realize that we are way more different than it seemed to me at first. I mean, I need more quiet time at home and way less excitement or noisy crowds. Too much of such socializing and I'm a wreck! But it's okay... I just hope we both end up among like-minded people, doing what we love," the last words she drips out gently, to not hurt the other.

Silence, then Maggie coughs. "Whatever emotional roller-coaster I was on, you always brought a sense of okayness to me, made me feel like I was good enough, even special. Then Gregg came along and **Boom**: suddenly I needed stronger means. You're right, though, we do seem to want and need different things in life," she sniffles and blows her nose.

"Remember me in the future, when you're standing in the lime-light, melting hearts." Maria swallows a lump, "Let's check in with each other now and then: you have my number and address on the island, right?" They exchange bits of important info and finally wish each other well. After hanging up, her ear is red and burning hot.

Maria cries for a bit but with a feeling of closure. No one even mentioned Lori.

Sensing someone staring at her, she looks up. Jay's standing in the doorway, bathed in golden sunlight, with a ceramic cup and plate in his hands. His face is in shadow, still, it cannot hide that the almond-shaped eyes look swollen and his cheeks wet. The air goes out of her lungs. A relentless hand squeezes her heart.

How is she ever going to cope without him?

~ Twelve ~

Slumberland

This trainee position is a disaster; dear mother of mercy, why did she let her parents talk her into it!

Or is it perhaps perfectly normal to hate every second of your workday? Shying away from your employer, the saturnine Mr. Applegate, while humoring as best you can your politely smiling, drowsy-eyed co-workers as well as the bargain-hunting customers. Maria's busy bearded manager has the body shape to suit his name and never gets hers right but keeps calling her Mary. He is the head, almost religiously overseeing the bedding department at this huge retail chain, selling beds, mattresses and all things bedroom equipment, most often at a discount.

"Welcome to Slumberland, Mary," in a painfully tight grip, he shook Maria's hand, "regardless of our trade name, slackers aren't welcome, but I can tell you are of the right kind!" She smiled vacantly. How he came to that conclusion was beyond her.

The sharpness of the many fluorescent lights in here, on top of a wall-to-wall carpet sending out a chemical stench, give the new apprentice a throbbing headache. The constant dulcet muzak sounding from the loudspeakers doesn't help, either. Maria's anxious face peeks back in the restroom mirror; her eyes look like big balls of lead. Now and then they, involuntarily, show the white. She quickly splashes water on and rubs them.

Hopefully, no one noticed her sneaking away?

She's stolen a moment to herself again, in desperate need of a respite in her tasks of neatly arranging piles of bath towels and beddings, followed by filling up big steel containers with pillows of varying sizes and quality. Maria gets an uncontrollable urge to crawl into the middle of one of them: the perfect cover! If only she could stay in there for the remains of her workday, peacefully observing the commotion from her fluffy cage. It's not like she's wholly here, anyway...

Arranging bedroom equipment is nonetheless a walk in the park compared to when Maria's boss tells her to help out at check-out. She hasn't figured out how to work the cash register, yet. Panic rises, her heart races and her mind betrays her when she needs it most. Maria shaky-handed tries to hit the right keys while a more or less impatient; at rush hour often grumpy, customer stares straight at her. The glowing red numbers become a blur: the angrier the glare, the more clumsy and vision-impaired the trainee gets. Maria's never been the best at thinking on her feet and gets frantic. Her old hardwiring takes over.

This is brutal.

At first, her co-workers, many only slightly older than her, smiled sympathetically. But after a while, their smiles turned to mild annoyance as they, once more, show her how to use the tiresome thing. By now, they've resigned and largely let Maria off the hook. Working the cash register's part of her training, but they often kindly let her organize the shelves or arrange things along the aisles, instead.

Turns out, there are quite a few tricks of the trade to this task, too. Tricks, like perfect product placement, how to lure customers to buy as much as possible. It's a science.

The bedding store is part of Slumberland: a world-and-wide-spread retail chain that planted its flag on Matter Island decades ago. At Maria's mother's workplace, they deliver standard-sized curtains to the local Slumberland situated in the near vicinity, hence the workshop-owner, Lilian, knows the manager here.

A retail trade training is always useful: an appropriate starting point for a young woman on the brink of adulthood. Particularly one with nowhere else to go and who needs a paycheck as Maria's father pragmatically stated one autumn evening, after bringing the matter of her month-long unemployment up at dinnertime, "You need to get a proper job."

The smell of wood he brought about, so similar to that nice scent at her grandfather's workshop, was the only sweetness present and not enough to stop Maria's heart from sinking. She tensed up, uttering a few feeble objections. The words got stuck in her throat.

"It's so kind of Lillian," her overly explanatory mother cut in, "and the store is within biking distance; scarcely five miles away. You can borrow my old bicycle for a start. I know this is not what you were hoping for, but we all have to be realistic, Kitty cat. Making a living right out of high school, especially in the Arts, is rare. Apprenticeship in the creative field is hard to come by, even in the city, whether one's talented or not. And as we know, college is out of the question…"

They don't say it out loud, yet Maria senses being in an unflattering light, now. How she's done a fine job of squandering a unique opportunity for a small-town girl…

Dad mostly speaks calmly or neutral, while mom will often sound pitying.

Do her ears pick up on, even if well hidden and vague, a note of gloat in any of their voices or is that preposterous? It must be, because both faces only reveal the usual. After all, being right is reassuring and leaves your world unrocked.

At Maria's new job, slipping under her morose manager's radar is her biggest concern. That, and how to best prevent her anxiousness from going through the roof.

Sitting amidst a group of loudly chatting co-workers in the cramped canteen at lunchtime makes Maria quite nervous. Different energies and moods swirl around the room: some are having a falling-out, someone is secretly in love with a colleague. Everyday dramas. She tries to pay attention, strives to engage in or at least keep track of small talk and banter about family life, sports, Tv, anniversaries and the likes. It tires her, though.

People genuinely care about this stuff, so why doesn't she? Be that as it may, the load of superficial information soon gets too much, triggering her squirrely tendencies.

Complying with workplace politics, some unwritten, is another headache. At Fairview, the general conduct was based on empathy, kindness and common sense. An atmosphere of trust helped foster seamless human interactions.

Fitting into a pecking order, even if clear cut at Slumberland, at times escapes Maria. To make sure there's always plenty of coffee available is for instance considered the apprentice's obligation. Once, Maria forgot to make a new pot of coffee after pouring herself the last drops and subsequently, all hell broke loose as there was no stimulating hot cup of joe ready for Tammy and Maureen by the beginning of their coffee break. At yet another incident, Maria made the stuff too weak for their liking. To avoid any future hassle, she hangs a detailed note in capital letters about it on her locker.

Maria quits drinking the blasted beverage herself: caffeine amps up anxiety, anyway.

She does sometimes have a nice chat with Silvia: a warm-hearted middle-aged woman who recently became a grandmother and so keeps flashing pictures of her chubby-cheeked grandson to anyone who shows a tad of interest. Often Maria skips lunch, settling for cookies, a candy bar or, at best, an apple in the locker room. Lunching on her own actually feels less lonely. She feels increasingly disconnected, like was she floating in space, tethered to earth merely by the thinnest of cord, fearful the cord, any day, might break.

Moving back to Matter Island was beyond disappointing.

A dimensional nosedive similar to the dive her grades took last year at Fairview with Margaret replaced by Jeanette and Maggie gone. She lost touch with her creativity, forced to use all her resources on managing the emotions brought up. Since she came back, Maria's muse has downright deserted her. Or maybe it's the other way around...

Here, there's no welcoming committee for it.

Maria's too busy, trying to stay clear of a vortex of darkness, sucking every shred of light into its black abyss. To claim such a maelstrom of misery only pertains to Mag would be a lie. She knows it well herself and right now has to do all she can to avoid its gravitational pull. Every day, it's at the forefront of her mind. Unescapable.

At nighttime in Maria's old bedroom, enclosed by all her mother's sewing tools, she whispers over and over into the ether that this situation is only temporary. Soon, she and Jay will surely come up with a better solution, or maybe Helen and Christian will. Or even Ray.

She recalls Helen's comforting words when the two of them had a heart-to-heart on her last night at The Meadow Muse, "Self-discovery takes time. Only a lucky few know what their vocation is early on in life: in reality, it can take years, even decades, of trial and error. I've read your script and don't doubt that you're onto something. Don't give up!"

Maria felt so low, she couldn't help weeping, "I feel like such a failure. Just keep it."

Helen stroked her tenderly down the back, "Listen, as I know a little about where you're coming from and the whole wretched situation: this is **not** your fault, sweetie. Patching up early wounds and making up for lacks in childhood takes a long time. I can only imagine what kind of silent inner battles you've been fighting all along. Remember that most of your classmates were not..."

Though the realization was bittersweet, Helen's validation did warm a lot. She craves it now where there's a shortage. Maria mustn't forget her soul family in the city.

She's not alone in figuring things out.

Eat what's on your plate

"Maria, didn't you hear me: dinner is ready!" the motherly call cuts through her offspring's train of thought.

Her daughter, who got off work less than an hour ago, is resting on her bed. Hands folded behind her neck, she stares into space. Outside, it's already pitch dark. Inside, too. It's been a loathsome burden of a day. Yet another one. Reluctantly, the pensive young woman gets on her feet. She's not the least bit hungry. A packet of digestive biscuits is lying on her nightstand with only half of it left. Her stomach is full and mind and body pleasantly tranquilized.

In the kitchen, an odor of minced meat makes her queasy. Her dad piles potatoes on his plate next to three big meatballs and drowns the whole heap in a sea of dark brown gravy, shoveling it all in with the greatest pleasure. For show, Maria takes a bite of her one meatball, followed by a mouthful of potato. The gravy is thick and sticky.

John is staying at his friend, Bryan's, house, Maria's mom informs. The constant chatter of her, eleven going on twelve, buoy-
ant brother usually dominates the air at dinner but not tonight.
It's quiet except for the sound of chewing.

"Had a good day at work?" mom breaks the silence. Her husband nods, still chewing, her daughter looks up and puts the fork
down. "Uhm, today, I made a mistake at the cash register," she
half-smiles in a light tone, "I corrected it, as soon as I found out
the amount was wrong. It was only about a small change: the customer got his money," she hurries to say. "Oh no, Maria! I trust you
told your manager straight away so he could fix it? If you don't get
money matters right, it's crucial to call on your superior!"

Maria nods, swallowing a lump. Of course, mom is upset. She
shouldn't have said it. Trying with all her might to prevent water
from welling up her eyes, she peeks at her father for reassurance.
He's too busy devouring the food on his plate.

More silence, then her father finishes chewing: "Was it someone from our village?" Maria shakes her head. "Don't worry then,
these things happen all the time," he winks at her, the tone nonchalant as always. His daughter picks at her meatball.

"Eat up, Maria, don't be so picky. I trust it tastes okay? The
expiration date was yesterday but the meat seemed too good to
throw out," mom starts fretting, shifting her full focus back on her
spouse as usual; face anxious, eyes questioning. Maria and her father nod in sync. To her mom's satisfaction, dad pours himself a
second helping.

None the wiser, Maria follows suit with only a slightly smaller
portion.

Doing the dishes, mom and her talk about trivial matters. Maria chats, breezy despite her belly ache, about this and that to fill the void left by her little brother. Afterward, she retreats back to the sewing room to rest. She then reads for a bit: the local public library has, thank goodness, proved to be a saving grace for her after she came back. Soon, Maria falls into a deep sleep. Bone-tired, anxious and utterly blue, she wakes early next morning to yet another dark and excruciatingly long December day.

Christmas is coming on in two weeks, and by the day, the number of present-chasing customers increases by hundreds. Slumberland is turning into a nightmare. There's no place to hide, everybody is needed to get through the Christmas shopping flurry. The manager is ever more short-tempered, the staff: sapped service-minds on auto-pilot.

All these gifts people buy need wrapping and who better than Maria, who easily gets overwhelmed, to handle an additional task that works well with a singleminded focus.

This task starts out a breather.

One of her first customers is a young woman with long wavy hair and gentle eyes, who has bought some beautiful bedding in a botanical design for her little sister. "Like me, Lucy's got a soft spot for flowers," she smiles. "Me, too," both of the young women's faces light up.

In Maria's chest, a tightly closed sunflower opens one of its glowing petals.

"Oh, maybe your sister would like a drawing on her gift card! What's her favorite flower?" the words escape her lips before she's able to stop them. "I'm sure she would love that," the kind customer seems thrilled, "well, Lucy adores tulips." Luckily, it's a simple one. Maria makes the bow extra pretty, too, and hands her the present with the hand-drawn card attached. "Wow – thanks!" a grateful smile on the sweet lady's face makes the artist feel happy.

After that success, Maria begins spicing up a lot of the presents by adding a personal touch. She puts on extra ribbons to create a spectacular bow, adds a little drawing or even writes a tailor-made poem; much to the delight of the person on the receiving end. She starts feeling confident, thinking she's finally found her niche: home safe. For a while work is play.

Alas, Maria's newfound joy only lasts so long.

A few days later, the store is yet again crowded. Maria hardly notices the bustle. She's tuning it all out, fully focused on getting a bunny rabbit right on a gift for a two-year-old obsessed with bunnies. The toddler's aunt looks on in awe. Maria draws a few delicate details and the woman asks how on earth she does it? Enthusiastically, she starts explaining how, when someone taps her on the shoulder. Maria peeks up.

"Ahem; maybe you could teach art class on your own time, Mary? If you have time to spare, there are plenty of tasks waiting for you...or perhaps you think your co-workers should carry the load on their own?" even if his voice is lowered, the belittling tone fits the stern look on their manager's face. Maria's stomach drops as does the pen from her hand. "S-sorry..." she stutters, aimed at both of them. Frozen, avoiding eye contact, she hands the customer back the gift card with a half-finished drawing on it.

Only three other customers are queuing by the gift wrapping table but the last one does glance at his watch a lot. Her fingers pick up their pace. The robotic doll is back.

Back to busyness as usual, Maria's gift-wrapping expertise is the only thing benefiting from the ever more stressful, hazy race until Christmas. Increasingly, she'll get ordered about to wherever there's a need for a helping hand. Her vulnerability and weaknesses are constantly exposed, Maria feels. Even if trying her best: after a few days, she just can't adapt any longer and hiding it is hard.

A sea of uncried tears wells up inside in waves too big to ignore. Maria's drowning.

The most precious parts of her alternate between shut-down and melt-down; every minute, she struggles to look the part; keep up the appearance of a together person.

How much longer can she pull it off?

Checking out

"Open one more counter, for crying out loud!"

The gray-haired woman in an oversized, black duvet jacket standing in the middle of a long line of customers doesn't hide her aggravation, "This is taking **forever** and with an unused counter just sitting there... I have to get to the bank before it closes!"

Silvia rubs her aching temples. She's an experienced and angelically patient cashier whom all customers love; however, having been at it for ten hours straight, even she is worn. Nearby, standing by the gift-wrapping table next to Customer Service, Maria ducks her head, doing her best to make her work look indispensable. Alas, to no avail.

She senses Silvia's eyes land on her, searching for somebody to lend a hand. **Anybody** apparently, even the last resort.

It's nearly closing time on the last day before Christmas. These final days, Maria has been wrapping and wrapping and wrapping a little more. By now, she's become a pro, much faster than any of the others and even gained a bit of acknowledgment for it.

"Maria, you're needed at check-out, pronto!" even if expected, the dreaded call from the loudspeakers startles her. Her lips start tingling and fogginess overtakes her brain. She was hoping for a break to grab a bite; hasn't eaten for hours. Instead, she drags herself away from the wrapping table and over to the empty counter next to Silvia's.

The angry customer has already switched check-out line and dropped off a huge pile of various goods. Pulling out cash from a square wallet, she flashes a big amber ring. The woman stands waiting, impatient and ready, long before Maria drops down by the cash register. The apprehensive apprentice clumsily stubs her toe in the process and the unexpected pain sends a shock wave through her system.

Something about the woman is familiar. The ill-fitting duvet jacket hides most of her figure; she's wearing glasses and the perm is a little shorter, but the leathery face and piercing eyes are unmistakable. It's Elsie from the village: the, literally, old fishwife, back from the days of the fish factory.

The surface of Elsie's black overcoat seems to absorb all surrounding colors.

Maria uses all her willpower on raising her gaze to focus on the woman's sagging face. Elsie doesn't recognize her in workwear: Slumberland sweatshirt & matching cap. Maria sees the thin lips move but can't make out what they say even if the old hag is close to yelling, probably something cutting or a rant about the service, here. With an elbow lifted to mitigate her fall, she lands on the anthracite gray carpet.

Merciful, soft darkness dulls her senses.

"Wake up, Maria!" A waft of wind brings her back to Slumberland reality. Maria finds herself placed in an armchair in the manager's office, not knowing how she got there. Silvia's warm eyes are full of worry. She's standing right beside her, using the store's Christmas catalog as a fan.

Mr. Applegate, with an odd yet becoming facial expression of fatherly concern, shows up behind his employee. He wipes his forehead, revealing a sweat stain under the arm. "All customers are gone now, the store's closed," he states, "what's the matter, Mary; haven't you had enough to eat, today? And what about fluids? It's important to drink extra water at stressful times, you know that."

"I guess, I haven't," Maria sits up straight, ashamed about her shortcomings. "Who filled in for me?" she looks at Silvia. "I took over while Sil and our maintenance guy carried you aside," their manager reassures. Silvia drops down in another chair beside Maria, "Thank goodness, the holidays are here, eh!" Maria nods, feeling better.

Mr. Applegate clears his throat, "Ahem, on a side note, I realize, not everybody is cut out for the demands of this job. Once in a while, an apprenticeship fails... maybe you and I should have a chat about finding another placement for you when the store opens up again after Boxing Day?" Maria is on the brink of tears, "Okay."

As far as she knows, only the simplest of tasks like unboxing new goods, tidying and cleaning are left. On one level, she truly would prefer it, on another, can't gloss over the failure. Avoiding Silvia's eyes, she excuses herself, saying she needs a sip of water.

Maria stumbles to the restroom to collect her shattered self.

After hastily wishing her co-workers Merry Christmas, Maria steps outside on this chilly winter evening. It's blistering cold tonight. She pulls the orange beret Ray gave her at her farewell party well down. "Cover your ears with this if the islanders talk rubbish to you," he said mushy-voiced. Ray'd taken her little jest seriously and hence washed the beret; though foolishly at a too high temperature: it didn't fit on that full head of hair any longer. Still, the sentiment touched Maria a lot.

Each morning, the small ritualistic act of letting her eyes feast on its fiery hue while holding it and then putting it on, sensing the warmth of the fuzzy wool helps the anxious apprentice get by one more day.

Maria's fingertips go numb inside her gloves. Trembling, she unlocks her mother's big black ladies bike, turns on its lights and rides home with feet barely able to reach the pedals, however heavy they may be. A thin layer of ice on the water in the old country road's potholes crushes beneath the wheels.

Maria lets herself be anesthetized by the cold, overcome by a familiar frost.

The perpetual loser has lost the spirit of Christmas, as well.

Seizing the day

Maria is a pro at other things than gift-wrapping.

Throughout the following holidays with the unavoidable traditions and innumerable rituals, no one notices anything different. Having moved back to the island, she is no longer of special interest and right now Maria's happy lying low. All the while, there's a hole in the pit of her stomach, not even her grandmother's rich and plentiful cooking can fill.

The incident before Christmas was merely the last straw. For months, the desire to break free has been growing strong inside Maria. On Boxing Day's Eve, she calls Jay to run the matter past him. They haven't spoken since Thursday night.

He has a lot on his mind, though, since grandpa Ray had suffered a minor stroke last week: a huge shock for all of them. "Oh no!" the cold hand squeezes Maria's heart hard, "but...but just this summer he was as sprightly as ever! Is he okay; when was it?"

"Friday around dinnertime, I think. He was, thank goodness, together with grandma when it happened and she called the ambulance," Jay's voice is shaky.

A flash of what else happened that day springs to Maria's mind: a spooky coincident?

Over Christmas, Ray has recovered some, but he's still hospitalized. "There was no holiday festivity at the cottage this year. Grandma's in a state, of course. We've had a somber Christmas, running between my house and the hospital. I've been meaning to call you but simply haven't felt able to..." Jay breaks down, crying. Starkly sensing her friend's emotions, Maria comforts as best she can then allows herself to join him in his sorrow. They sob together, clutching their phones.

A virtual hug traveling through way too much space.

After a while, their sadness softens and Maria tells Jay about the downhill turn in the short story of her work life. "I'll just pack it in; can't make it through one more day!" It goes silent at the other end, so long, Maria, for a slow-motion moment, fears the connection's lost. Then Jay's back on the line again, saying he finds Maria's intent a little risky, but that he feels bad enough for her to support it.

"I swear, Matter Island is not a place: it's a state of being. A real downer! Don't worry, I'm sure, everything will work out for you," Jay's faith in her has always been stronger than her own. "Let me know how it goes - I believe in you!" the cheer is welcome.

The day after Boxing Day, Maria's father, as usual, drives off to the carpentry at half-past six in the morning. She, too, is up early for work. She puts on layers of clothes, as usual, packs her lunch-box: some cinnamon cookies and an apple, as usual, and waves her mother goodbye with a forced smile as usual.

Not everything is as usual, though.

With a few tweaks suggested by Jay, Maria's desperate, disjointed thoughts have grown into more of a plan and today is the day for it to be hatched. She sees no other way.

It's raining, but the light drizzle feels refreshing after being stuck inside for days among all of her chatting, feasting and smoking relatives. Her parent's old boiler has, besides, finally collapsed and they've just bought a brand new gas-fired one. This heater is recommended by Mr. Price who's used a similar one for years. Although he, of course, needed the most extensive heating system the company provides to be able to heat up his huge house. Gas heaters are efficient in cold climates such as on Matter Island and thus widely used. Half of the village has one.

Dad calls it nonsense and mom says she's exaggerating, but Maria is certain she now and then detects a vague stench of gas in the living room, adding to a stifling sense of airlessness indoors.

Today, that long bike ride to her workplace suits her fine.

When Maria arrives at Slumberland, blessed by a brisk wind at her tail all the way, she is, for once, the first one there. The day is dawning. It's only half-past eight: the store will open in an hour. Perfect timing.

At the staff entrance, she shaky-handed unlocks the back door for the first time ever. Like Maria, each member of the staff has got their own key to the back door while only Mr. Applegate or similarly important people are trusted with ones to the front of the giant building containing the store itself, a few offices and a large warehouse area.

Inside, the locker room is harshly lit by neon lights but relatively warm. It smells of rotting apple in here. Someone's left an apple core behind in the trash bin after the room was cleaned. A pang of conscience. No, she ate her apple at lunchtime, Maria relieved remembers. Staying on the bench for a bit, she goes over what she's planned to say, feeling colder with each passing minute. Will he accept it?

Their manager's office is located further down the hallway, right before the door into Slumberland. The sizable room has a big window wall overlooking the store so that he can keep an eye on everything and everyone but shaded so no one can snoop on him. This is where he summons people who are to be sacked like a poor bloke was in Maria's first month here.

The clock says ten to nine, she's right on time. Mr. Applegate always turns up earlier than the staff, at least half an hour earlier, she knows.

Maria's heart gallops. Still, the blood doesn't circulate properly through her body: the extremities stay numb. She rubs her hands together and stomps her feet to make them come alive. Every ounce of strength and vitality is needed to do this; that familiar, seductive sense of inertia has to go.

Five minutes later, the headlights of a car briefly illuminate the shades. He is here.

When Mr. Applegate sees Maria standing in front of his office, he halts for a second then slowly approaches, "Good morning, Mary – gee, you're at it early, today! Did you enjoy the holidays?" he sounds sleepy but the niceties roll smoothly of his tongue.

His plotting employee plays along, "Yes, I did - thank you. Uh, about that word, you said we needed to have; could we have it now, please?" Maria's voice trembles slightly. She straightens up, looking at him with a flickering vision. "I guess we could..." Mr. Applegate stares surprised at her. He unlocks the door and steps across the threshold, waving her along. Inside his room it's airless, bordering suffocating. Her employer clears his throat, opens a window and sits down by the large mahogany desk, nodding to the same chair she sat in a few days ago. He puts a pile of papers on top of his desk. *Christmas Sales Report* the upper one says.

Maria inhales some mouthfuls of fresh air under his brooding tawny eyes. She folds her hands firmly in her lap to hold them steady. It also serves as an anchor, keeping her present where she's at, not drifting off into space. At last, she speaks.

Reciprocating the niceties, she asks him about his Christmas, but halfway through, the blasé look on his face has her quit trying to make a personal connection and cut to the chase.

In a daze and floundering, until helped by the fire of desperation, Maria hears herself express all the things she's been longing to communicate since the beginning. Words like: "unfit", "unwell", "wrong for me" and "artistic introvert" are flung around. Most words are her own, the fancier ones, Jay's. Lord knows if any of it makes sense...

Mr. Applegate's face, a mask of surface courtesy, hardly ever changing except for the occasional temper flare, reveals little sentiment during Maria's speech. The mask is impenetrable, her heartfelt explanation and wordy sentences fall upon barren ground. The flurried adolescent gives up on being understood and tries a third approach: speaking his language.

"To say it like it is: I wish to cancel the apprenticeship. I'm not able to stay any longer. The usual one-month notice, unfortunately, doesn't work for me, and as the holiday season is over, I'm certain you can easily get by without me right now. If you just pay me for the working days up until Christmas, including the extra hours, it will be fine by me. I hope that works for you?" Maria leans forward with an expression intended to be questioning which in reality is pleading.

With a grunt, her employer leans back with one hand resting on his belly. The mask briefly slips away, and he stares at her as if she was a sad, likely neurotic, peculiarity.

"So, you want to depart Slumberland already? Certainly, no one is forcing you to stay. By all means, if you've discussed it with your parents and really think you can make it in the Arts, plenty of young people are eager to replace you. All right; I'll let you go and make sure your last paycheck arrives shortly. Hand over your key, please." Maria does as told. With a deploring hand gesture, Mr. Applegate rises to show his former employee to the door, "Godspeed then, Mary!"

Maria hesitates for half a second before turning around to, long-overdue, correct him. The door is, however, already shut close. She grabs the door handle: locked.

Once you've fled the gates of Slumberland, there's no going back.

On the bike ride back, Maria's co-workers gawk at her from their cars in passing. Silvia honks the horn and the ex-apprentice waves to her, smiling impishly. The rain's gone, and it looks like the sun will make an appearance; even the wind is settling to ease her journey.

The world has, in spite of the season, switched back to color.

~ Thirteen ~

A bike ride back in time

The cold air only feels refreshing as she pedals onwards.

There are quite a few hills to conquer on the way back from Slumberland. In high spirits, she even takes a detour around the harbor to look for traces of change. Down there are no signs of life, except for crying seagulls. They're probably disgruntled by the sight of all those keeled over fishing boats: how there's no longer left-over fishy morsels to snatch.

Maria bikes past Mr. Price's palace-like place with its excessive number of rooms. She notices condensation on some windows, also suggesting it to be an out-of-proportion amount of square feet to inhabit for one man and his only progeny: overkill, indeed.

The mansion itself, with its towerish shape and arched paned windows: some even barred, reminds her of a castle from the Middle Ages. The jagged steel fence around his huge garden doesn't quite fit the bill, though. Not like a moat would!

As opposed to Price's plot, many village gardens, like Maria's parents', are enclosed by a blue-painted wooden fence or the alternative: a white picket one, making for a, even if somewhat dated, softer expression. Unless you try to climb one, of course, in which case the pointy pickets suddenly turn to teeth; tearing your clothes or delicate skin.

She knows from experience...

When Maria reaches the crossroads right at the last hilltop, she, as usual, catches sight of her parents' house by the end of her childhood street, right before driving out of Ferrysville. Everything looks exactly the same. The blue-framed windows are dark.

Instinctively, she hits the brakes and jumps off.

The harbor and Slumberland are far and well behind her. Standing at the junction between two diverging roads, Maria inhales a deep and invigorating breath. She lets her throat open fully and her lungs receive pure oxygen; a sensation both pleasurable and a little painful. Before her, the letters on two brand new road signs glow starkly red, lit by the rising sun.

Mini Market, one of them says, the other one: Recreational Area.

With deliberate movements, Maria turns the bike around to take off in the opposite direction, away from the Mini Market and her parents' house. She rides purposefully fast to outpace any second thoughts, towards the new recreational zone to the east of the village.

Summer's Bend emerges. Nostalgia hits her, and she slows down in passing. A smile lights up the young woman's face. Her cherished childhood refuge seems to be the elemental piece in a settlement of other, newer summer-houses, loosely scattered across meadows and moors, each home sheltered by birch, fir and pine trees. As of right now, the scenery's subdued with the sun emerging over a hazy waterline in the distance, all newborn, red and quivering. As soon as this summer, the setting must be lush and scenic: out of this world.

Someone has renovated Summer's Bend. The cottage practically shines from floor to roof; brought back to and even beyond former glory. "FOR SALE", a sizable sign in the driveway says.

Maria parks the bike against the old water well which the owner has graciously let stay. She walks around the house, admiring the good handiwork. Feeling sentimental, she lifts her gaze to look at the winter-clad garden. The old swing set is, strangely, still in there. Maria sits down on one of the swings, gently stroking the oak wood, lingering. Softly rocking tho and fro, the joy of her five-year-old spirited self slowly comes alive. Exiled parts of her reassemble themselves, brought back by echoes of a summer past.

Maybe a soul never forgets its true belonging?

She shouldn't get ahead of herself, though. This was only part one of her plan: part two awaits.

The hardest part.

As far as apron strings permit

Boldly, Maria decides to take the bull by the horns.

When she comes back after her joyride down memory lane, both her parents are still at work while her brother is at his friend's house: John's second home these days.

The enlivening bike trip has given her just enough courage to face her folks. Time's ruined until it's done; better get it over with. They're going to discover it soon, anyway.

First off, and just as well, is dealing with her mother who still works part-time. She usually gets off the bus at half-past one. There's no light on in the kitchen as of yet.

The coast is clear.

Maria carefully sets the table and makes a hearty lunch. Even brews a pot of coffee, too: a perfectly balanced one, she makes sure. Definitely a more delicious meal than that of her mom's usual packed lunch! She feels okay calm and confident. Prepared.

"What in God's name are you doing home so early?"

Maria's mother's worried face combined with the shrillness of voice, nevertheless, shake her daughter's composure. "I've made lunch, mom; I hope you've got room for more," Maria smiles appeasingly. The seamstress takes off her jacket and drops the handbag, staring befuddled at her offspring. Sunrays play with the sensible, short hairdo and silver threads Maria hasn't noticed before, shine among the blond. Dark circles under her anxious blue eyes, newly formed tired lines: her mom looks frail.

Despite the youthful appearance, her mother's getting older. The young artist's resolve begins to dwindle, replaced by guilt-ridden insecurity. An equal opponent is easier to handle than a fearful child, masking as a mature adult.

"What's going on, Maria? Are you feeling poorly?" Being sick is the only reason for leaving work early, her mother can imagine.

An overwhelming temptation to go along with the assumption hits Maria. She almost succumbs to it.

"I'm okay. That is, I'm fine now, but I've been feeling unwell every day at Slumberland since I started. I'm simply not cut out for that sort of work, mom!" the desperation shines through even if she does what she can to prevent it.

Maria's mother goes silent but not for long, "You think I am so excited about going to work every day, striving to meet certain standards already set out for me? Then let me tell you: I'm not. I like my job, but on cold, dark winter days like today, would I prefer to stay home, too, doing my own thing? Of course! That's normal, that's how it is; we all have to stick it out. Adults have to go to work, have to earn money somehow, just ask your father. Do yourself a favor and stop being so difficult!" After the habitual fretting has subsided, Maria's mother gets wound up about having to repeat such an obvious point to her adolescent offspring.

Is she a little dense, maybe?

Maria slumps in her chair. It's a lost cause: mom will never get it. She's on her own.

This is the reason she started off with Mr. Applegate. Had she done it the other way around, her plan would've stranded before it began. No doubt about it, her instincts served her right. And she just **couldn't** stay. City life has irreversibly changed her: it's broadened her mind and made her aware of other possibilities, other ways of life. Like most people, her mother thinks her beliefs are truths, though. By now, they're firmly cemented; have become her reality. Most folks here stick to what is known.

From now on, whatever will be, will be.

The laminated tabletop blurs before Maria's eyes: the emotional intensity's too much. An old nodding doll takes over. Her mom mellows, patting her complicated kitty cat on the cheek. "Christmas is over: from now on working at Slumberland will be easy as child's play! Um, looks yummy," shifting to a lighter tone, her mom grabs a piece of bread and reaches for the butter. Knowing it'll never ever be *her* idea of play, Maria starts eating, too, letting chunks of bread help her swallow the lump in her throat.

Soon, she excuses herself, saying she still feels under the weather.

A bit later, Maria sobs facing flat down her mattress, muting the sound in the pillow. Her body trembles as a tidal wave of built-up frustration, fear and sorrow, all muddled together, blase through her.

"Don't resist it, let it flow," her favorite teacher's calming voice resounds in her head. Midway through the squall, her own mind comes on board, and she has the wits to lock the bedroom door. Mom protested when Maria asked for a key, claiming she needs to be able to get hold of her sewing tools. Her daughter, for once, didn't back down; now, a blessing. Mom's barged into her room without knocking before...

When the storm finally calms, her pillowcase is soaking wet. How much water does a human contain? Maria hates crying, but Margaret says holding it all in is potentially damaging, besides way more painful. Recent experiences confirm this to be true...

"Everybody has a message to convey, preaches their own perceptions and beliefs. It's okay. Keep trusting your own heart and senses. After all, any sensitive child is born in tune with that which lies beneath: the spirit moving the matter. Let others forget but you stick to that."

Claire's gentle guidance soothes her frazzled nerves. She rests her head on the pillow.

Outside her window, snow is falling. Dressed in white, the island looks so innocent and serene. Quite the cover-up...

- Maria sweeps the blue paint across the last patch of raw wood on the fence. Anxious and utterly exhausted, she takes a step back to examine her work. In doing so, the painter instantly shrinks to the size of Thumbelina. Horrified, she discovers this to be her normal size here. Now, the fence suddenly grows, looking enormous; mounting, not only high above her but also stretched as far along the horizon as her eyes are able to follow. In fact, the fence encircles, not only her parents' plot but every last bit of Matter Island which towns, fields and roads, she now notices to be covered in snow. Everything is white if it isn't blue. Maria is as well, even her right hand with its white knuckles and crooked fingers, like a blue hook holding the paintbrush. It's a dismal sight. Did she really do all of this!

Margaret materializes beside her, gazing at Maria with eyes as wise and old as earth itself. "Stop, dear," her voice loving as ever, "the fence is done but may soon be gone."

A flicker at the periphery of her eye. She turns towards the movement. At first, she cannot make sense of what it is. It does seem to have human outlines; has Mr. Freeze finally caught up with her? Chills. Then she notices that the figure glitters or glistens. Silently sliding closer, it grows bigger. Oh, it's Maggie! Her soul sister looks luminous, glowing and sparkling in all of the colors of the rainbow.

Mag shines from head to toe, the frozen landscape springing to life in her wake!

Maria lifts her gaze to the gable of her parents' house. The huge clock is still there. But wait; there's no ticking and the hands of time aren't moving. The clock's stopped and with that, the awful sense of urgency fades away: impending doom is dispelled!

When the weary young woman wakes up, she feels the spark of life return along with a marrow-deep resolve of no longer holding herself back. Maria understands that this no-man's-land she's currently in is only the very beginning.

She **is** back on track.

Budding breakthroughs

Mom's knocking on the bedroom door: "Dinner's ready, Maria!"

At dinner, Maria's unscripted lunch isn't mentioned, and the next day the supposed apprentice is up early and heads winter clad out the door, as per usual.

Half a mile from home, she rides down a side road at her left: a shortcut leading to the harbor. Once there, she heads straight east, toward Summer's Bend and the other summerhouses.

Maria parks the bike against a fir tree and for nearly eight hours braves the elements; strolling on the beach or wandering the potholed dirt roads and narrow forest trails. She explores cozy cottages, peeks longingly through windows and eats her humble lunch sitting on a wooden bench in someone's snowy garden. Once, she hastily hides behind a pine tree when an unexpected resident, apparently on a prolonged vacation, shows up in his doorway. Later, a sudden hailstorm has her seeking shelter in a shed.

At dusk, Maria, cold, tired yet reluctantly rides her mom's bike the same route back again. This procedure is repeated on the following day. Likewise, the day after that.

Many a night, Maria and Jay, whispering, discuss the predicament; weigh her options.

"I wish you could come and help me out... As you just said: Ray is back home again, undergoing rehabilitation: doing okay under the circumstances. Why don't you come for a quick visit, Jay? We could go see old childhood spots: Summer's Bend, too. Your old cottage looks absolutely amazing now!" the wistful words slip over her lips. Words she's been holding back because of Ray, besides knowing very well how Jay feels about this place.

In desperate times, a girl may have to stoop to devious measures.

Jay goes quiet then sighs; "Maria, there's something I have never told you.... Ahem; even if I was only six back then, I still remember it," his voice gets low and thin.

"Uh, your father, for some reason, felt threatened by my mom. Even at six, I sensed it. One time, he and I were briefly alone in your kitchen. You had gone to the bathroom, I think, while I was sitting at the bench, drinking a glass of lemonade. He drank a beer and ate some sort of fish by the kitchen table. I thought it smelled icky, I recall.

After you'd left, he peeked over at me. Um, I clearly sensed he didn't think much of me... Then he asked: "So, your mom; does she like being back in her hometown?" I nodded and he went on, in a weird, husky voice: "It must be so different, living in a small town compared to a big city full of people. I'm sure, she's got company at times. You guys have guests sleeping over once in a while, right?" there was a strange smirk on his face, I didn't like. Before I could say anything, your mom walked in, chirpily telling him off; how maybe I would like a taste of the fish, too, which I quickly thanked no to. Then you, luckily, came back..."

A sense of ickiness rises from Maria's belly to her throat. Torn, not knowing what to say, she wishes she could unhear his story. Let the curtains remain closed on this part.

When she doesn't speak, Jay goes on, warmed to share more delicate subject matters:

"And that's not all. Some of the kids in town bullied me... That Bill chap with the hunched back: by the end of our stay, he and his chum were always on my case, calling me stupid names whenever they saw me!" there's anger in his voice which is a rare occurrence. "I know Ferrysville is your birth town as well as my mother's but besides meeting you, I honestly don't have that many fond memories from there."

Maria finds her voice again, "Oh, it wasn't only you, Jay! Bill bullied me and others, too. Most kids in town were afraid of him. He could always find something to pick on. He had a tough time at home, though: alone with his crazy cold father. After the skating accident, I told you about, and after hooking up with Susan, Bill changed."

"Well, if you say so... I'm sorry but I don't particularly feel like rushing back to the island to see if you're right!" Jay snorts. He goes silent for a moment before sighing, "All right; since you obviously need me there, of course, I'll come..."

Maria bites her lip, to not scream too loudly with delight, "Appreciate it, thanks, Jay!"

They decide it's probably best if he visits her some time in January; just for a few days or a weekend. Maria promises she'll have spoken to her parents before then.

In the middle of everything, Maria bumps into her old classmate, Milly, at the Mini Market. Milly seems more confident these days, and she invites Maria and Stella to a New Year's celebration at their house. Actually, it's her big sister, Molly, throwing the party. A lot of old pupils from the village school will be coming: a bunch of teenagers and young adults.

Stella's clearly psyched about this reunion, and Maria sees no way out of accepting Milly's kind invitation.

On the fourth day, the day before New Year's Eve, the head of the family has half the day off so that he can go pick up his wife and son after lunch: a family shopping trip is planned. Mostly because the Mini Market doesn't sell fireworks as of yet, much to Maria's pre-teen sibling's discontent.

"Bryan's dad already bought a huge bag!" John loudly implores. He obviously knows which button to push: dad can't bear his little boy lacking anything other boys have. While his son will be more than ready at noon, his daughter is believed to still be in Slumberland then...

That morning, the snow's almost melted, a glowing sun is rising and there's even a whiff of spring in the air when Maria rides toward Summer's Bend. High above her, thousands of stars slowly give way to a mightier radiance. The vista today is stunning and the sight for a moment quiets her anxious, racing thoughts.

A twinkling ignites in Maria's mind. Yes - Claire is back!

*What if failures may very well be fortunate and even adversaries possibly helpers, pointing you in the right direction? What if time really **is** your own, if only you dare to believe so?*

Heading down to the beach, Maria invites further details. Mirroring the outside sun, a glowing ray rises like a pillar of warmth and light inside. A new passion project is called for!

Maria loosens her grip to lift the gloved hands from the handlebars. Victoriously stretching her skinny arms up in the air, a distinctly girly yet never-before-uttered cry leaves her winter pale lips. The sound sings triumphantly across sleeping meadows.

She then lets her shoulders relax and arms rest comfortably at her sides. Maria knows her mom's clunky bicycle, by now. Keeping balance and steering with her body come surprisingly easy.

The last stretch, she drifts delightfully among evergreens and barren-looking fields where the growth layer just below the crust is readying for spring.

When she comes back, the rest of the household is still out buying fireworks.

Luckily, Maria's already got hold of her own.

A paycheck with a pricetag

On the 31st of December, Slumberland's closed.

Today, the escape artist can sleep in, unquestioned, wiped after one whole week of keeping out of sight, biking and wandering about outdoors in the middle of winter.
It's still been ten times better than the alternative.

"Wake up, Maria! I need you to explain something to me!" an agitated cry-out from her mother abruptly pulls her out of her innocent slumber.

Instantly, Maria knows what's going on. She just didn't think the letter would arrive this soon; not until next week when she can check their mailbox herself, first. Oh no, she isn't ready - darn it! Ready or not; here comes the dreaded "Big Talk"...

"I'll be right out!" still half asleep, Maria drowsily rubs her eyes to look at her watch. Gee, eleven hours of drifting in dreamworld. She must've needed it.

Dressed in the morning gown mom gave her, frayed after years of use, on top of her flannel pajamas, she drops down on her chair by the kitchen table. It seems dad isn't home which is only a relief. His absence is probably for the best.

Her mother, fully dressed in a warm woolen sweater over a blouse, sweatpants and thick socks, holds a letter up in the air. The clothing is sensible since they had to shut off their new gas heater yesterday after John sniffed something fishy, too.

"I took the liberty of opening this letter, not realizing it was for you..." mom's eyes are wide and worried. Tense, Maria looks up. The envelope, not surprisingly, says "Mary" on the front. For most, though, this misspelling would hardly cause confusion. To be fair, mom's never seen any of Maria's paychecks since Mr. Applegate has handed them over by the end of each month ever since the start.

A familiar sinking feeling hits Maria. Frowning, she nods before carefully taking the opened envelope out of her mother's hand and pulling out two sheets of paper. She starts reading them. It turns out to be her last paycheck and a release paper from the company; she has to sign it on a dotted line next to Mr. Applegate's signature. Maria doesn't even think to take a look at the amount.

The fog of Matter Island arises again, messing with her mind. Her tongue, too; she feels her mouth go dry.

"Look at me, Maria! What's going on?!" while the words are expected, the acidic tone physically hurts. Teary-eyed, the teen daughter meets her mother's glare. Mom's face shifts into an ex-pression of alarmed pity. Inside those widened blue pools a reflection of Maria is shown; ever so small. That's how her mother has always seen her and the exact mirrored depiction of how mom measures herself.

On reflex, Maria shapeshifts, habitually shrinking to fit her measuring stick.

There's no way to control it: a waterfall of tears pours from the teen girl's eyes and loud sobs from her mouth; her throat aching and tummy contracting with each one. During the storm, though, at the very core of her being: it is ever so still and silent. Right there, a loving, all-knowing presence is witnessing, certain everything is okay.

A knowing that she's okay, as she is. Even amidst this out-of-control, emotional mess.

Maria's mother has no other option than to wait. She sighs profusely with her head askew. Her face mellows some, shifting to one of childlike confusion. "There, there," she reaches out and strokes Maria's hair, "don't be so emotional, girl! Maybe if your father phones Mr. Applegate on Monday and asks nicely, they'll allow you one more try and let you come back; maybe doing mostly manual labor?"

In the middle of a sob, Maria inhales deeply. Jay shows up in her mind's eye, staring at her with those fine eyes: tender and expressive; yes, but also eyes expecting respect.

She straightens up. "NO, I am **never** going back there," she asserts. Her no is firm.

Of that, Maria is certain. A pillar of warmth shoots up through her spine. The flannel feels too hot, all of a sudden.

Upset, mom grabs her daughter by the arm, "Are you completely **senseless**, child - apprenticeships don't grow on trees!"
she lets go to have a strengthening sip of coffee and in doing so
spills a splotch on the sweater which soaks it in right away, "Argh,
now look at that!"

She rushes to the sink to rinse the coffee stain out of the wool
fibers.

A bit of physical distance works wonders on the intensity of
Maria's emotions: the susceptible girl actually often wishes her
senses would lessen, "I'll work something out, something that fits
me better. I already have a few ideas. Which reminds me: I've been
meaning to tell you that Jay is coming for a visit, soon. The last
time we spoke, I invited him, figuring it would be okay with you
and dad since you've invited him yourselves before... It **is** okay,
isn't it?"

Mom turns off the tap, twirls around and looks at her, still
somewhat vexed, "Oh, **now** the young fellow finally has time for
us; certainly hasn't been eager to see us before! Then the usual ac-
quiescence takes over, she sighs, "He's welcome, of course. Helen's
done a lot for you. He can sleep in the living room or John's bedroom when he's out."

"Thanks, mom!" the relief of having everything out in the open
lifts a tremendous burden off of Maria's young shoulders. "Let me
remind you, that your father also has to know about your unfortunate behavior, Kitty cat," mom won't let her eldest off the hook,
yet.

The pillar of light transforms into a red hot ball in Maria's belly. "Fine. I'll tell him as soon as possible, but please stop calling me that: it's patronizing. I am **not** a little kid anymore!"

Be it her softspoken, submissive daughter's sudden frankness or her firmness of voice; mom is surprised. Her eyebrows rise fast and she smirks, about to regurgitate a line, uttered since forever from parent to child.

To her credit, her mother, for the first time to Maria's recollection, catches herself before blurting out her own childishness. She simply shakes her head.

Sitting down beside Maria again, mom sighs agreeably while removing a few pieces of lint from the flannel of the teenage daughter's p.js. She is, after all, still her mother.

Inexplicably appeased, mom nods with a sheepish face.

~ Fourteen ~

New Year's Eve

"Eek!"

A shriek pierces the airless basement; all the way across the grimy wall-to-wall carpet, echoing up the spiral staircase at the concrete back wall.

It goes dead silent for a second as if this room was no longer cramped with talkative, by now, far from timid young people. Maria flinches, aslumber on a bench under the stairs: it's the early hours, way beyond her usual bedtime. She sits up straight with a jerk, like most others staring nervously in the direction of the outcry.

The scream was made by Milly's twenty-year-old sister Molly: their dolled-up yet callow shindig hostess. Her face has gone pale beneath the make-up.

Somehow, the two girls' mother came down the stairs and entered the dimly lit room without Maria noticing. The sturdy, normally laconic woman clings to her eldest's skinny arm. Face flushing and eyes protruding, she lets out a rapid stream of words. Upsetting news, it seems. Afterward, she fast ascends the stairs again.

Weren't Milly's parents supposed to be away till tomorrow; invited like all of Mr. Price's former staff, to the grand, one-of-a-kind New Year's Eve Party/Handing-over Feast down at his mansion, tonight? Bill and Susan are the real planners behind the rare event which has been the talk of the town for some time. Certain guests have even been offered an opportunity to stay the night afterward in one of the mansion's many guest rooms. Maria's parents are among the invited, too.

Price is certainly serving his fellow men a different kettle of fish, these days...

During a confidential chat earlier in the evening, Milly mentioned, that her parents were going to take him up on his offer. "Dad says, the old man owes us way more than a measly overnight stay after mom's been slaving for a pitiful pay at his factory for decades, but a small compensation is better than none," Milly's eyes shone in the dark. Parroting her father's sentiments, Milly sounded so unlike her insecure self, that it took Maria a minute to grasp what the girl said. The dumping ground owner slash used car dealer standing up for his hardworking, chain-smoking wife is, nonetheless, somewhat hard to imagine.

Something is brewing in the village...

Maria's stomach churns as goosebumps spread across her skin. Her heart pounds fast. The numbing effect of the beer evaporates all at once, and her fine-tuned sensory system reacts, as always prepared in a split second in case a catastrophe should occur.

Molly violently hits the light switch, and crass light from three neon lamps in the ceiling pierces the party room which, even if currently covered in New Year's Eve decor, quickly reveals its true condition. "Sorry, guys: the party's over! Mom says there's been an accident at Mr. Price's house tonight," her voice cracks, "oh my god, is he really dead?" Molly, known as a high-strung lass, gasps and puts a trembling hand in front of her mouth.

The other teenagers huddle around their hostess, hungry to learn more. Maria looks over at her old classmate Milly, who remains stiffly on the chair she's sitting at, only clutches her seat and stares at her mother and sister. In a daze, Maria gets on her feet and walks over to the small crowd. She tries to make sense of things as everybody talks at once in a dramatic fashion like the emotional kids they still mostly are.

"But how? I know he was no spring chicken, but Bill told me only last week, that the old guy had a good many years left, their doctor promised," a lanky boy from Molly's class wants to know. He leans forward with a furrowed brow and arms crossed over an underdeveloped chest. Molly shakes her head, she doesn't have all the details, only that there was a heated argument with a lot of accusations thrown around right before it happened: it was too much for poor Mr. Price, apparently.

A hush falls over the room as the group simultaneously realizes that life as they've known it is over. Sure, change has been at the doorstep for a while, yet this unexpected passing is a prominent sign of a collapsing powerhouse of the past. It highlights, beyond doubt, that a new, brighter future is near.

For the tender youth, the party in the basement is over. A time of uncertainty and unfamiliarity awaits: of unprecedented events mixed with baffling blessings.

Tearing down the staging

As Maria walks through the mud-colored, winter-barren village on her way home, there's a deep, deep stillness in the misty air. The silence is palpable, enveloping every brick house she passes in a hush. In most houses, lights are still on but some subdued red and violet stripes at the horizon show promise of a bright day to come.

If the sun is able to clear this fog.

At first, the quietude feels unsettling, like a foreboding, but by the end of Maria's journey, her strides in silence have cleared her mind, calmed the frayed nerve ends and brought her whole being into a welcome state of peace.

It's been such a strange night: she hasn't slept for more than maybe an hour. Neither did Milly, her rattled sister or Molly's long-time girlfriend, Jill, who stayed over, too.

After the party crowd had finally left, the sisters talked their mother into disclosing further details about the incident at Price's place. With her husband away, the woman went ahead without re-straints. What she told them, kept the teenage girls awake for most of the night.

The evening started out fine. Bill and Susan holding hands, joined by the old man, acting agreeably from his wheelchair, wel-comed their guests at the mansion entrance. They were then led into a sizable hall with a huge mahogany stairway to the 1. floor and a crystal chandelier hanging from the ornamented ceiling.

The villagers, who for the most part never had been inside, were oohing and aahing as they were shown around the giant house. A house with, to match its exterior, decor much in the style of a castle from a faraway Golden Age: heavy damask drapes, golden candelabras and framed portraits abound.

In particular, Elsie was in awe, declaring such regal décor was to die for.

Finally, the guests were led into a large dining room that looked more like a chamber and got seated. Almost all the adults from Ferrysville were present; all except for the elderly or sick. The mayor of Matter Island was there, too, as well as some officials and other important characters from Price's past. There were people from all walks of life, an assemblage of high and low.

Bill seemed on edge as he invited everybody to the table. Mr. Price nodded graciously and the feast began. Overawed, the villagers hardly spoke at first. Only after several mouthfuls of exquisite cuisine and a glass of expensive wine, did people start to loosen up and enjoy themselves.

Milly's mom hesitated for a second. Her usual, expressionless face re-surfaced, and she exhaled with a deep sigh. The four girls, sitting on the edge of the household's well-worn velour sofa, sent her encouraging nods, eagerly leaning forward.

Thus incited, the unlikely storyteller continued:

"All around the table, people were acting chummy with each other, tattling, laughing and joking. Old feuds seemed forgotten. It was quite nice to see. Then maybe a few hours after, Bill clinked his glass: time for a speech from the household son and heir."

Milly's mom inhaled and started speaking in a confidential whisper. All ears, the girls scooched closer.

"Bill was pretty plastered: he had to hold on tight to the back of his chair!" leaning back, the two sisters' mother let out a rumbling chuckle through yellow teeth.

She picked up a cigarette from her bag, lit it and after a long drag, blew out a big puff of smoke. Maria scooched a bit away.

"Poor guy; he was clearly too drunk but determined to do this speech... And it started off okay: a lot of thank yous to this and that. First, Bill hurriedly thanked his father for handing over his ships, despite his initial skepticism. We clinked our glasses, cheering. Then he made a special heartfelt toast to Susan and her family for making him feel welcome as their soon-to-be son-in-law."

That's right: Stella was at Price's party, too; Maria almost forgot. Stella had grumbled, stating she would much rather celebrate New Year's Eve with the other teens but how she felt she had to help her big sister and brother-in-law out at Price's. Apparently, even the confident Susan was antsy and agitated, flurried about ensuring success.

Milly's mom went on: "People were listening and smiling, their stomachs stuffed with Price's grub and liquor. That's when it happened... Bill started talking to his father,"
she widens her eyes, pressing the lips tightly together, "now, I don't recall every word Bill said, cause he got wound up pretty fast. Never heard him speak so many words or so fast, and all about his loveless childhood. Susan pulled at his sleeve, in a hushed tone trying to stop him: "Billy, do you really think this is the time and

place...?" but to no avail. By the end, his face was all red and he was close to tears, **this** I remember.

Even if his son, it seems Price had always treated him like an insignificant underling, much like he did the rest of us. There was also mention of having the bruises to prove it... By then the poor lad was hard to understand. All throughout, Price just sat there with an uncomprehending expression on his face," the talkative woman paused and lit another cigarette.

"Um, to be honest, didn't we all kinda know the way Bill was treated wasn't right? Maybe not about beatings but on the whole," Maria heard herself say. Villagers did notice it, but still considered it within the normal, within the sanctity of family life. Maria now knows that what's considered normal on Matter Island doesn't necessarily means healthy. A sting of belated guilt. Females of different generations squirmed, exchanging a glance. Maria, who brought it up, came to the rescue, "Uh, I guess not many were actually treated well by him... What did people do, did anybody react?"

Milly's mother nodded, "Yes, some of the guests, mostly fishermen or factory workers from the village, were beginning to murmur heatedly amongst themselves. Your dad, as well," she gazed at her daughters who didn't look that surprised.

Molly fidgeted with her hair and Milly bit her nails which were now strong and long. Not like in primary school.

"You girls should've seen the mayor, though: he was completely befuddled, looking a right jackass!" the sturdy woman's raspy laugh flashes her teeth. She coughs and gets serious again, "anyway, Bill's accusations finally broke through his dad's thick skull or fog of medication - egomania; whatever it is that kept him from ever owning up to his crabby behavior!" the resentment oozed out of every word.

Evidently, decades of avoiding, at any cost, upsetting the apple cart are over.

"To be fair, the old guy wasn't able to do much to defend himself. His former minions turning against him in his own house while sitting in a wheelchair in that condition! He struggled to speak. People went quiet and glared at him, awaiting answers. Patrick Price lifted his right hand, usually an iron-fist, and let it hit the table, hard: "Get a hold of yourself, son! Emotions are for babies and out of control women!"

Some of the female participants protested. Elsie kept quiet for a change.

Patrick Price squirmed in his wheelchair, "You ungrateful lot: haven't I perhaps been putting food on your tables and roofs over your heads for decades!" More protest from Bill, besides from all sides of the room, now. Patrick inhaled, looking slightly shaken. Then he sort of collapsed in his seat. It went silent for a moment until he whispered, "Ahem, I'm surprised and sad, Bill, that you see things this way. I realize the necessary women I brought home, in the hope one of them might become your new mom, fell short. Uh, I guess a mother's touch is irreplaceable. When she was... uh, gone, I couldn't handle it... The grief. Not to speak of... The guilt. Uh, I made up for it, the only way I knew how: by toughening you up as my father did me. I've worked hard all my life to make him proud: to honor him. It's what a man must do, isn't it? Could it be, I did you wrong...?" Patrick looked puzzled, "perhaps, I, at times, let my pain out on you, son... perhaps I let it out on all of you... if so, please forgive me," his voice got ever fainter. People were so quiet you could've heard a snowflake drop.

Suddenly, the face of the invalid man crumbled before our very eyes, and his upper body fell across the table. A few of the women screamed; we all thought he was gone. But Price was actually breathing fine, merely passed out. It had been too much for him. Bill got hold of a phone to call the doctor and afterward he and Susan as gently as possible wheeled his father into the old man's bedroom downstairs; one stair step at a time. The poor lad looked quite pale. All us guests were pretty shocked... After maybe twenty minutes, the doctor swung by to check on Price, soon assuring there was no cause for alarm, but to hold off on anymore emotional palaver; the old man was too fragile for it. He gave Price a valium, telling us to let him sleep till morning."

Never had Maria seen this chatty side to Milly and Molly's mom. The sisters looked mystified at her as well, listening intently, not wanting to miss a word. Jill and Maria gazed at each other, wondering: if Price was okay then, what killed him later? Instead of clarity, the plot had thickened.

Milly's mom gazed cunningly at the teens, hesitating for one last, long, second before revealing the cause of death. Not often had she known any such power, she wanted to savor this moment.

"Ahem... when Price was safely tucked in, the mayor and other posh folks went home. Your parents left, as well, Maria, to go pick up John at his friend's house, I think they said. Your mother, besides, seemed pretty upset about what had happened."

Maria nodded with a curvy smile. It sounded plausible. The storyteller went on:

"As for the rest of us villagers: we stayed, talking amongst ourselves for a good while. The near god we've all been serving for so many years was clearly a weakened, very vulnerable old man: a mere mortal. He's been crippled for some time, of course, but nonetheless: not until last night did the truth of things fully hit us..."

The chatty woman inhaled slowly to finally, with her exhale, present the plot point: "Gas is what killed him: Price was poisoned by a leakage of carbon monoxide from his own gas heater!"

The teen girls leaned back, gasping and staring at each other, wide-eyed.

Maria sent grateful thoughts to whoever or whatever gave her the sensibilities to notice and her dad the foresight plus willingness to turn theirs off. Only yesterday!

The terrible truth is that poisonous gas fumes from a faulty heater had slowly been pouring out; god knows for how long. The leakage must have been gravest in Price's bedroom, or perhaps he, at this point in time, simply was the frailest member of the household. Ever since his and Susan's engagement, Bill has, besides, been spending most of his time at her parent's house, leaving the care of his dad in the hands of shifting nurses and paid help.

After midnight and a bit of firework, the night nurse came by to check up on Price and Susan went with her. Most guests were about to leave the premises; it had been such an unusual night. The grocer's daughter was the one crying out when they found him unwakeable in his bed: poor Patrick had finally met his maker.

Stella ran in there and started shouting about smelling gas, and the women of the village who hastily huddled around his bed, sniffed and agreed. There was a moment of chaos. But Bill fast came to his senses and rushed down the basement to turn off their gas heating system while all of the guests ran around in a panic, hastily opening windows and doors wide on every floor of the mansion, from roof to cellar.

"As you can imagine, we were swift to blow out all candles!" The teen sisters' mother leaned her head on a pillow, suddenly looking wiped. After such a night, the heart of the house was naturally beat and needed to hit the hay.

It **was** quite a mouthful to digest.

The younger women followed her example. Except, the youth kept talking for most of the night, talking at length to get this nightly event and everything leading up to it, well out of their sensitive systems.

Later, when Maria walks past Price's place, the windows of the mansion are still open wide and so are its front door and steely gate. Apparently, no one's concerned about burglars despite, recently affirmed, reports of a huge art collection as well as numerous expensive belongings. How highly unusual: his house is transformed from a fort-like castle to an accessible buffet for any poor soul in need.

That nasty gas leak must've been substantial.

~ Fifteen ~

A Winsome vehicle

In disbelief, Maria looks around the bike shop then gazes wide-eyed back at Jay who's standing right next to her, smiling big.

The array of bikes in here is overwhelming: lady, men, kids, racing, city, mountain, sports and so on; each type available at varying sizes, price ranges and colors.

That last paycheck from Slumberland is going to cover for this bit of self-pampering. And not only for a new bicycle of her own: another key component in need of funds awaits. Those extra Christmas hours at the store were tough, still, she must admit the money's coming in handy now.

Everything is going to work out!

Maria didn't even know this well-stocked shop existed. It was actually Stella who, last Tuesday at the Mini Market, mentioned the brand new shop. And here it is, located on the northern tip of the island, in a village called Winsome. The small seaside town lies tucked in behind the brow of a hill in a small bay as far away from Ferrysville as you can possibly get without exiting the island.

To Maria, these are virgin shores.

Winsome is an undiscovered gem with its cute independent bookstore, a windy yet picturesque waterfront café called "Cuppa & Cookie" and arts and craft boutiques scattered across town. A charming speck on the Matter Island map; even Jay agrees.

The bus ride here took well over an hour. The old bus stopped, it seemed, every single minute, but since they were chatting all along, time melted away like ice cream on a hot summer's day. Sunshine peered through the dingy windows, revealing quite a few stains on the upholstery seats. A sunray caressed Jay's cheek and earlobe, highlighting locks of his red-golden hair. Poetry. Every so often, Maria had to lean forward and touch him to make sure he was real. Chuckling, he slightly shook his head, not minding too much.

Along with the weekend, Jay arrived yesterday in the late afternoon. Bleary-eyed after traveling by train for most of the day, he went to bed early and slept in this morning. Only now, is his awake, bright-eyed self beginning to re-appear.

After all these years, Maria almost can't believe it: Jay's really here!

Looking a little shyer than usual, he showed up at their doorstep carrying his worn backpack and a bag of gifts: one for Maria from him and one for Maria's mom for housing her son from Helen. The handwoven silk scarf in douce colors was well-received. The hostess oohed and aahed, shy as well, but eager to please and fussing even more than she normally does.

Maria wanted to wait till they were alone to unwrap hers: a gift tinkling slightly when she was handed it. Once in the privacy of her bedroom, she eagerly tore the paper off and a kalimba with a soundbox in oak wood adorned with a sunflower emerged.

"Thanks, Jay - it's beautiful! Uhm...what is it?" she had to ask, and he explained and then showed her how to play this small African percussion instrument, using one's thumbs. Its tones sounded soft and delicate, fast inducing a peaceful mood. Ahh...

Maria felt bad for not having a gift for Jay. Then she remembered, "I have an outing in mind for us tomorrow: a bus trip to a bike shop up north. I need a new bike, is why. Then I can also show you parts of the island you haven't seen, yet. Hope you're up for that?" Jay leaned against the wall with heavy eyelids but nodded, "Sure, after a good night's sleep, I'll be..."

John was out, staying at Bryan's house again, but right before dinnertime, her father came home. During the meal, this time not fish, an awkward silence arose. Her dad asked about the young musician's journey and how his grandfather was doing. After that, the conversation lagged. Dad's usual jokes fell flat. Maria couldn't help thinking about Jay's confession and neither could he, it seemed. Mom, bless her childlike soul, chit-chatted idly. For once, Maria felt grateful for her overwrought small talk.

Soon after, Jay called it at night, settling into John's cluttered, very boyish bedroom. Tonight, yet another bed awaits him: the sizable corner sofa in their living room. A mattress on the floor in Maria's bedroom would've been perfectly fine. "Your father won't like it, I'm sure. Let's not go there," her mother muttered when asked.

Anyway, seeing as Jay is finally here, better make the most of it. It's highly doubtful he's going to stay for long. Maria can tell just by having a quick peek at him whenever they're in the company of her parents. To her, Jay's face is an open book, giving every sentiment away: the good, the bad and the indifferent. It keeps her anxiously on her toes. It seems to be a book her mom can't read, though, and one her dad's only able to comprehend half of and thus scarcely can be bothered to flip through.

The reunited allies agree they need to get out of Maria's parents' house. They need to go somewhere they can be alone and converse, undisturbed, like on this northbound day trip. A similar hours-long outing must be planned for tomorrow. There's much to figure out, and Jay's leaving Monday.

Privacy is of the essence in finding the path forward to a favorable outcome.

By happenstance or a stroke of luck, Cuppa & Cookie is open on Saturdays, even in the middle of January. A coffee-sipping senior-citizen lady with a foreign face below bobbed grey hair is a lonesome customer. The view is spectacular, though, and it is homely, warm and delicious-smelling. A plump, cordial waitress comes rushing to take their order, besides light a candle on the red and white checkered tablecloth.

Silently, they stare out the window, cupping their hands around a hot drink of mulled wine alongside some crispy custard-covered waffles. The holidays are over, but Maria doesn't mind a chance to pretend she's, for once, celebrating Christmas with Jay.

"Sticky Waters" is behaving, today: the surface still and glassy, perfectly mirroring a few fluffy cumuli on an otherwise cloudless sky. The sound of seagulls.

Maria leaves a big bite of her last waffle, pushing the plate aside. Her sweet-craving has diminished since Jay's arrival. She's gained several pounds during the challenging last six months, and her skin's flaring up, too. To his credit, he hasn't mentioned or seemed to notice anything different, for which she's thankful.

By the looks of it, the city boy might also have gained a pound or two...

"I love that bike I chose: the frame was so light!" Maria looks him in the eye, "Yeah, a winner for sure, and the ruby red color suits you," Jay lights up in a dimpled smile. "There's still a chunk of money left; how to put it to good use? I do have an idea but before telling you about it, I would love to hear your suggestions, if you have any?" she sweeps locks of curly hair behind the ears and lets her chin rest in the palm of her hands, elbows on the table. Thoughtful, with her eyebrows raised and cheeks blushing from mulled wine, Maria gazes at him.

"Well, I actually also have a great one..." Jay's smile is secretive, "but something else first: I never got around to asking how your father took it when you told him you had quit the apprenticeship?"

Maria wrinkles her nose, "Urgh, I do my best to forget my Slumberland phase which is hard when it's only three weeks ago. I told dad, to be exact, on the 1st of January, on Sunday evening, right after Price died. He was somewhat softened since John and I may very well have been saving our family from a dire destiny. Although, he only listened when John said it... Chilling to think of what could have happened. Uh, our talk went okay, I suppose. Dad just said I need to find another source of income, soon. He had more vital things on his mind," she frowns, "there was still a great deal of hullabaloo in the village. All day, people gathered down by the harbor: dissecting, discussing and coming to terms with the situation. We returned our new gas heater on Monday; with complaints, of course. Same goes for more than half of Ferrysville's households. Suffice to say, the air in folks' homes will better from now on... And Bill's promised he's going to get the suspicious death of his father thoroughly investigated; he'll likely take it to court," Maria shudders, it's a horrid matter.

Jay seems lost for words, and she goes on: "Price's funeral turned into something of a mass meeting. Dad joked that half of the island was there but this is an exaggeration. It was awfully cold. Mom says it's always so at funerals, but this was brutal. The church was crowded yet still felt like a cold store, and people looked frozen. I had a hard time concentrating on the sermon, but finally, it was over. Then Bill, along with five other villagers, picked up the coffin to carry it to the grave. He looked pale then broke into a sweat; you could tell it was heavy. Price was a weighty man. I noticed that Bill looked taller than usual, and it confused me. Then I realized, his hump seemed to be gone and his back as straight as the other pallbearers'..." immersed in the memory, Maria shudders again and slowly puts her winter coat on.

"The Wake, in contrast, was homely and heartwarming."

Dethroning one last tyrant

Maria peers into the candle flame.

Outside, dusk is creeping in: the sun has set. A few minutes later, she wakes up from her thoughts in a jolt. Like in a wave of dominoes, Maria's sudden movement continues through Jay who also straightens up in his chair. He looks at her, awake.

"I've got this idea, I can't wait to share! Here goes: what do you think of me becoming an art teacher?" she stares at him with wide eyes, pressing her index finger to her nose.

"Uh, only for small children, like kids in kindergarten or primary schoolers, of course. Do you think I am good enough for that?" Maria leans anxiously forward.

The idea was, unwittingly, gifted her by two adversaries: Jeanette and Mr. Applegate.

Jay scratches his neck, "Sure, you are! Great idea, Maria, **plus** it fits perfectly with one I have in mind. Believe it or not, the idea evolved out of my grandma's concerns about what'll happen to their cottage after grandpa's stroke. Even with months of training, Ray's unlikely to gain his full strength back," he folds and unfolds his napkin.

Jay puts it aside, it's his turn to lean towards Maria, "Why don't you come live at The Meadow Muse this spring? Grandma told me they have to sell a big portion of their land, and how she hopes to keep most of the garden. Even after that, they're going to need someone to take care of the cottage and what's left of the plot. Mom and dad are too busy working in the city to do it, and so are Lisa and I. If only you are willing to maintain the place, you wouldn't have to pay rent but could pursue your creativity: your art, writing - teaching, whatever you like! I'll gladly swing by and help out, too. What do you say?" Jay trips over the last words, his eyes sparkle in the cozy, candle-lit café. He casts them down, "I miss you, you know..."

"Wait... what?" the new bike owner is flummoxed, but Jay isn't finished speaking yet, "Mom has besides, in usual undaunted fashion, taken matters into her own hands," he picks up a pile of papers in his backpack, laying it on the table under Maria's nose. Her final term project! Jay nods encouragingly, as she reluctantly flickers through the script. A bitter taste in her mouth. There's a letter tugged in at the end. "For Maria" it says at the top.

Dear child,

Hearty greetings from an old friend, now basking in the blazing sun at a warmer climate.

Reading your sensitive short story has been such a treat, Maria! Then again, I always knew you had a treasure trove of rich and soulful expression inside you, yearning to be set free.

The poignant and deeply poetical way you worded the familiar yet fragile human experience touched me and made me squeal with delight more than once. I see so much promise - please keep at it, darling!

If you want me to, I would feel honored to be amongst the first ones to read the next writing from those gifted young hands and sensitive heart of yours. I would love to accompany you on your writers' journey if you'll generously allow me to?

Wishing you a joyful future of soul fulfillment,
Margaret

A dam bursts in Maria's chest, the water streams down her reddening cheeks. Oh, she loves them all so terribly much! How could she even begin to deserve such kindness?

Her head starts spinning.

Guilty jubilance. The letter brings her monumental joy, not to mention envisioning Jay's suggested scenario. If only based on other, better grounds, because how can she be pleased about it **now**? And what will her mother say about her daughter leaving her, them, again...? Jay still gazes at her, waiting for an answer. Patiently, he tilts his head. From his face, she can tell he gets what's going on inside.

Jay reaches out and grabs Maria's left hand, right as she's lifting it to bite her nails. "You don't have to answer, yet. Just know that Rose would be so glad and grateful to have you, there. And don't worry so much about your mother: trust me, she'll get by... Having you there would make all of us happy, but what matters, first and foremost, is what would make **you** happy, right Maria?"

What makes her happy? To be truthful, Maria does know now, deep down. A stirring in her soul touches scar tissue of a barely healed wound. It hurts.

This surely is too good to be true. She can't bear yet another disappointment or even worse: have Rose or others be disappointed in her. What if it's all too much for her?

Her vivid imagination runs amok, picturing the cottage in the middle of night with flames licking around its windows and blazing through the roof because she, absentminded, didn't shut the stove properly. Wooden houses catch fire, like, in a matter of seconds! Next up, an image of the garden looking like a bombed battlefield after a minor war comes to mind. It's not like Maria's ever had the green thumb; not like Ray or Rose.

Making art and writing, of course, sounds beyond amazing, but can she really claim to be a true artist without an education? And what does she even know about teaching; no formal training or anything!

The candle flame dies in front of her eyes. Darkness falls upon their table.

Maria comes to her senses.

Still somewhat perplexed, she looks up at Jay who's been painstakingly observing her. A flash of his teeth in their dimmed area, "Please allow people who care, to help you. Maybe the pickle isn't so much getting you away from this old island as it is getting its devious or, at the very least: doubtful, ways out of you?"

Exhaling, Maria lets her shoulders drop. He is right.

Margaret once proposed the world serves much like a mirror reflecting our inner light as well as shadow parts back to us. So that we have a chance to see it all, delight in it or mend it. "Always be open to learn but let go of the habitual self-doubt and second-guessing yourself. Have faith in your particular spark of life: what feels true to you," she softly added.

It was too mind-blowing to understand back then, but Maria thinks she gets it now.

Her dreams can come true if she's able to accept that the road leading to them will look different and the steps she must take, in reality, likely will be messier and also a measure more mysterious than envisioned. A road of learning and growing. Healing.

Thanks to previous schooling, she masters the basics. And to do what she is naturally made for doesn't require any degree or particular piece of paper or fitting into any pre-defined role. She could simply let go of the endless striving to be acceptable and desirable: to feel good enough in the eyes of the islanders or even the world at large.

It's a confidence trick.

Looking only at external parameters, she seems thwarted at every turn; wings clipped. Yet leaning on faith in herself as well as the One who created her, she's free to fly, freed by grace from the grading hell of society, needing no additional permission slips or rubber-stamps of approval. If only Maria intends so and allows for it; rather than crumbling or turning to dust, what has often felt like a minefield of darker emotions could metamorph into a flourishing field of creativity, yielding ample unique artwork.

The sunflower in her chest opens all of its glowing petals at once. "I would absolutely love it: tell Rose I'm ready whenever she needs me there!"

The young artist's face lights up in a wide smile as she imagines steering her shiny new ruby red vehicle down the forest trail, Unity Path, towards the beloved cottage.

Confident, steady on her feet and from a centered place, she steadfast threads the bike pedals while the horizon expands before her eyes. The sweet scent of honeysuckle and wild roses tickles Maria's nose, a choir of merry meadowlarks accompanies her every move. Trees and green fields abound, days of discovery and unbridled joy ahead.

The designated direction is clear. It's time to embark on her own unique journey!

It's time to head homeward.

EPILOGUE

As dated defenses defrost,

melting set snowflakes of past

Mirasols miraculously birth:

Heartlights shining on Earth

ACKNOWLEDGMENTS

First, I wish to thank my dear family who kindly provided me a nesting space while I wrote the better part of this novel. I so appreciate your help.

Once more, I send grateful nods to countless authors of fiction, psychology and self-help books, whose words were a wellspring of wisdom; way too many to mention. I also, once again, want to give thanks for all the other resources I've been blessed to have access to. From supportive online communities to other types of, often free, online content: apps, articles, videos and courses, etc. - the true boon of the internet.

My warmest thoughts to everyone who's kindly shown interest in this book or in any way helped create it.

Last, but not least, heartfelt thanks to my beloved muse for not letting me down and likewise to the Creator behind all of creation for bestowing me a calm container in uncertain times so I could keep writing.

* Despite searching, I haven't been able to track down the name of the author of the quote on the bathroom wall in chapter eight. The source seems to be anonymous.

ABOUT THE AUTHOR

Mona Kristensen is a Danish fiction author: an intuitive writer passionate about depth psychology and dream work. She has a keen eye for the subtle ways in which Life speaks to us and a deep love of Mother Nature. The healing of the most open, sensitive, expressive and imaginative parts of us is very dear to her heart, too: vulnerable aspects that sadly often end up wounded or repressed. Through her work, she aims to mend a bit of this unfortunate damage.

Mona's hope is that her writing may validate, empower and uplift fellow sensitive souls as well as help raise awareness on deep-seated issues many struggle with.

Her book series: "Becoming Maria" is out now.